"What about love, Mr. McClain? Isn't that the most important consideration when two people make a commitment to a relationship that will span fifty or sixty years?"

"Look around, Miss Stacey. Lots of folks fall in love, but they just as easily fall out. I'm willing to bet on natural chemistry and deliberate choice. We've got the chemistry. All that's left is the choice."

Now he reached into his inside jacket pocket with his free hand and Stacey saw the small flash when he brought it out. There, circling the tip of his index finger, was a simple solitaire diamond on a gold engagement band. It was simple, but elegant, and she was experienced enough with fine jewelry to know it cost a fortune.

"I choose you, you choose me."

A wedding dilemma:

What should a sexy, successful bachelor do if he's too busy making millions to find a wife? Or if he finds the perfect woman, and just *has* to strike a bridal bargain...?

The perfect proposal:

The solution? For better, for worse, these grooms are in a hurry and have decided to sign, seal and deliver the ultimate marriage contract...to *buy* a bride!

Will these paper marriages blossom into wedded bliss?

Look out for our next CONTRACT BRIDES story, coming soon in Harlequin Romance®!

BRIDE OF CONVENIENCE

Susan Fox

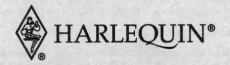

TORONTO • NEW YORK • LONDON
AMSTERDAM • PARIS • SYDNEY • HAMBURG
STOCKHOLM • ATHENS • TOKYO • MILAN • MADRID
PRAGUE • WARSAW • BUDAPEST • AUCKLAND

For Joanne Anderson

ISBN 0-373-03788-0

BRIDE OF CONVENIENCE

First North American Publication 2004.

Copyright © 2003 by Susan Fox.

Visit us at www.eHarlequin.com

Printed in U.S.A.

CHAPTER ONE

THE lady was broke.

She was dressed just as richly and stylishly as before, but this time in a sleek, shimmery teal designer original that showed off her blond coloring and perfect body. She looked like a million bucks, but she was worth little more than a few thousand dollars.

He was here to change that.

Oren McClain had taken on a losing prospect or two in the past. Mostly ranches or abused horses. He had a modest gift for spotting potential in some failure or misfit. The right management or backing or retraining might turn a respectable profit or reclaim something of value. Or bring it out.

The willowy blonde across the room carried a few of those little potentials that always got his attention. He sensed her quiet desperation as she nursed yet another glass of wine.

Everyone else at the crowded penthouse party was too self-absorbed to see the shell-shocked dullness in her pretty blue eyes. None of them would have realized that her talent for regularly getting the waiters to bring the drink tray around for a discrete exchange of empty for full was partly the need to anesthetize herself from the pretentious bores and tiresome elites at this big city soiree. She might be too snookered to let herself realize it, but he knew she would later. He meant to point it out as bluntly as possible, if need be.

There was a weary intelligence in those lovely eyes, along with a dispiritedness that could be expected of a woman bored out of her mind with her shallow, aimless life. A life that had spoiled and sucked almost everything worthwhile out of her. That's what happened when life held no greater challenge than could be met by beauty and a charming smile. Or a hefty tip.

And yet it was clear she was in mourning for the shallow privileged life that was rapidly coming to an end. Oren McClain was certain he was one of the few at that stuffy penthouse party who knew Stacey Amhearst's days of bartering beauty and charm, and bestowing hefty, persuasive tips wouldn't last another week.

But *she* knew it. Which was part of the reason she looked morose and standoffish. And panicked.

He'd learned a lot about her in the past few months, so this wasn't idle speculation. The lady truly was broke. Her spacious apartment and all the other costly doodads that went with it suddenly had the shelf life of Beluga caviar. All the beautiful, wealthy snobs around her who didn't already know, would very soon find out the jarring truth.

And then the invitations would dry up. Most would stop taking her calls, stop reading her phone messages. Their butlers and maids wouldn't answer the doorbell or, if they did, they'd recite some polite little fib to deny her entry. She'd be the hot topic of gossip as they nattered to each other in hushed, horrified tones, as if leery of attracting the same unthinkable misfortune.

Most would be eager to put her downfall out of their minds and move on. As if forgetting her quickly and pretending she'd never been part of their rarified society might somehow inoculate them against contracting the same terrible fate. Fate like bad luck or bad investments or embezzled fortunes, along with the poverty, and the shame and shock of being shunned by peers.

A few of the men, both the single and the unfaithful married who appreciated class and education and beauty, might come her way and offer some sort of arrangement, respectful ones or not, but those would fall through. He'd see to it.

Oren McClain hadn't come back to New York after all these months because of some paltry bit of business. He'd got wind of her trouble weeks ago, but he'd stayed away, waiting for a pampered thoroughbred to lose a few more important races and show up at sale where she could be had for a song.

The flashy little high-stepper who'd danced, delighted, and set his blood on fire, then kidded him about his marriage proposal, hadn't taken him seriously. She'd thought the things he'd offered her were nothing more than the quaint exaggerations of a Texas rube too inflamed by his libido to be telling the truth about what he could provide for a wife.

She might see him in a different light now. After all, she'd need someplace to go after next week. Texas would be as good a place as any for a woman who'd had her privileged life stolen and was about to suffer the abandonment of peers.

And once he got her to Texas and she learned something about how to live a useful and satisfying life, she might even grow to love him.

She was half finished with her latest glass of wine, and had just located one of the waiters to watch for a chance to give him a subtle signal, when Oren McClain started toward her.

As a farewell party, it was a crashing failure.

Perhaps that was because few suspected it was a farewell party. She might as well have stayed home.

Stacey Amhearst quickly changed her mind

about that. It was depressing at home. She couldn't pretend anymore that it was cook's night off, or that her butler had gone out to see his ailing mother. She'd come here for comfort and edible food.

There was little comfort to go with the food. What had she expected? That her pedigree-obsessed friends would crowd around sympathetically and offer to help her raise money with a charity auction? She really would throw herself in front of a limousine if anyone but her closest confidants found out about her outrageous misfortune before her lease was up on Thursday.

Was it better to live in an embarrassed state in financial exile somewhere, or let everyone think she'd tragically died rich? The fact that they'd only find out later that she was a pauper had helped her to squelch that fleeting thought of limo-cide.

Actually, she'd been half hoping for some conveniently rich man to sweep her off her feet tonight and fly her to Vegas for a quickie marriage. Her reputation for spending money would have made it easy to conceal a ploy or two that would funnel funds into her accounts. After all, she had plenty of expensive clothes she'd never worn publicly that hung in her closets, and some off-the-rack things still sported tags. With a little imagination, it would be easy enough to pass those off as new purchases. If her conscience allowed her pride that much.

But one of the problems of the sophisticated set was that for the few people in her circle who did marry at her age, an ostentatious ceremony with all the pricey traditions was a requirement for a first marriage.

And there was no unattached single man here tonight whom she hadn't already mentally crossed off her list of potential husbands, so there could be no quick trip to Vegas.

Bad nerves and depression had left her with little more ambition tonight than to fill her stomach with rich goodies and numb herself with vintage wine.

She didn't care for alcoholic drinks of any kind, and rarely imbibed. Until tonight. Tonight was her farewell party. The last fling on her social calendar before she ran out of money and lost her place among the only people she'd known.

And then she saw him.

At first, the very tall, brutally masculine rancher from Texas seemed merely a phantom that fear and desperation had conjured up to haunt her.

She deserved to be haunted by her memory of him. She'd not treated him particularly well at the end, but she'd been so disrupted by him, so very threatened by his earthy masculinity and the shock of the things he'd made her feel, that she'd been compelled to protect herself.

She'd regretting rebuffing him almost right away. She'd tried to smother her guilty feelings by telling herself that he was too honest and straightforward—too *real*—for her. A real man like him would find out soon enough that she was too frivolous and inept for his way of life. How would a man like him react when he found out? She couldn't bear his bad opinion. She'd rather be thought a snob than a failure.

Even worse, he owned a cattle ranch somewhere in a dusty corner of Texas! She'd be useless and lonely and bored out of her wits. The only thing they'd really had going between them had been the explosive physical attraction that had so frightened her.

None of her friends knew that she wasn't at all as sexually sophisticated as they were. In fact, she was so sexually unsophisticated that she was still a virgin at twenty-four. She'd been quite happy waiting for the man of her dreams and her wedding night, though most of her friends would have laughed at that old-fashioned notion.

Then she'd met the cowboy, and he'd overwhelmed her so badly she'd been terrified. She'd never told a soul about him, because she'd known she would have been tittered over and teased about it. Either because he was a rancher from Texas or because he was so macho and rabidly masculine and unrefined—or because she'd been so turned on that she'd panicked.

Hadn't she met him here at another of Buffy's parties? It had been months ago now, and she'd almost made herself forget. That's why it was such a surprise to think about him now. He'd been someone's guest, but she doubted she could remember who because she hadn't paid attention when the introductions were made. Her brain had short-circuited and she'd had eyes only for the macho beast. Everyone else had vanished from awareness.

As Stacey watched her delusion, appreciating the beautiful cut of his elegant black tuxedo, she felt her pulse begin to accelerate and realized it was the first time in a long time that her heart was beating fast because of excitement rather than fear.

McClain—yes, she still remembered his name—wasn't handsome, but he was striking, with a charismatic masculinity that a lesser male could only dream of having. It was such a pleasure to watch her delusion walk toward her in the safety of her imagination that she delayed the sip of wine she'd been about to take.

And then her delusion stopped in front of her and neatly plucked the wine flute out of her cold fingers to sit it with absent aplomb on the tray the waiter had just brought. His other hand settled hotly on her waist and she felt the jolt that told her this was real.

The cowboy was here.

He was so tall, built so tough and hard, that his lean frame was solid with muscle. She realized again that he wasn't at all handsome, and noted afresh that his rugged features had the kind of weathered tan that hinted at Native ancestry as did his overlong black hair. His eyes were a glittering black that went perfectly with his coloring and the costly cloth of his tuxedo.

His low voice was a gravely drawl that called up images of a sexy night in bed.

''I've been waiting to dance with you, darlin'.''

Stacey felt the room tilt a little as he expertly eased her into a private corner nearer the door. It didn't matter a whole lot that they were the only ones dancing to the soft notes of *Unchained Melody* that the pianist on the other side of the room was playing.

Suddenly, just like before, they were the only two people in the universe, and Stacey felt her head spin with the idea. Was she tipsy or had the pressure and upset finally caused her to snap?

The heat of him was scorching, and the rocky hardness of his big body made her knees tremble.

The hand at her waist rested boldly low on her back, and the shivery pleasure of being wedged snugly between that hand and his body was almost erotic.

"H-how did you get here?"

Her brain was so fuzzy that she wasn't completely certain he was really here, but somehow his first name came out of the fuzziness: Oren. It was a Southern name. A good one for a cowboy, but hopelessly out of fashion.

His stern mouth curved faintly. "The usual way. A pickup, two planes, a taxi and a taxi."

Her soft, "How did you get in?" sounded dazed. Again, he obliged, and her gaze fixed on his mouth.

"Just like last time. The visiting guest of a guest."

Stacey's brain somehow seized on the notion of second chances, and she almost missed what he said next. That was because she was looking up at him and they were dancing slowly, which made the dizziness worse.

"I came to New York to see you."

The words struck sweetly for a few seconds, but then turned bitter. What would have happened if she'd accepted his crazy proposal months ago? She wasn't clearheaded enough to catalog all the horrors and disasters she might have been spared, but she knew if she'd married him then, at least the loss of her fortune wouldn't have caused a fraction of the shame she was in for now. At least she wouldn't be six days away from homelessness.

"Oh, why?" It came out sounding forlorn because it was the start of the questions that were suddenly revolving in her mind: *Oh, why didn't I marry you?* And, *Oh, why was I such a fool?*

"I had to see if things had changed for you."

His words made her heart give a sickening lurch and her head was suddenly heavy. She let her chin go down and her gaze fixed on the snowy white between the facings of his jacket. Her eyes were stinging and she bit her lips together to hold back the emotion that was coming up like sea swells.

He went on speaking as if he hadn't noticed her reaction.

"I thought I might spend a few days, take you out, see what you think now. Unless your answer is still no."

Stacey realized she'd placed her hands on his chest and that they'd slowly stopped dancing. It felt for all the world as if they were still moving, because the room was moving.

"I think I'm not feeling well," she got out. She couldn't get her brain to come up with anything else. Mostly because it was the truth, but partly because she should have told him "no." *No, I haven't changed my mind,* or *No, because I'm no better suited to a life with you than I was before.*

Either would have let him off the hook. It would have been kinder to disappoint him for the second time now, rather than later. But she'd felt too desperate for some kind of reprieve or deliverance for too long to automatically reject this potential lifeline.

That was the moment, despite all the fuzziness from the wine, that she began to feel guilty. Her guilt wasn't immediately acute, but it promised to be. Particularly since some survival instinct had kicked in and she suddenly realized that she might agree to almost anything to be spared financial disgrace.

The cowboy had said he was rich. That he had a big ranch and oil wells, plenty to keep her in jewels and designer duds...

Oh God, she remembered suddenly that he'd said that. He'd called them "duds." That had touched her then, and the memory touched her now. Touched her so much that she wanted to cry over the artless simplicity of a big, rough, macho man who'd seemed to be sincerely smitten and had made such a sweet, homespun offer to provide whatever it took to make her happy and choose him.

Jewels and designer duds... as if he was offering

his best to a woman he revered like a queen, but a woman who was so far above him socially that he'd never understand that a pretentious snob like her wouldn't be caught dead in a dud of any kind. Or married to a cowboy.

She couldn't seem to keep from remembering that he'd treated her delicately and deferentially, as if she was worthy of respect and pampering and perhaps even worship. She hadn't deserved a speck of those things from him then, and she certainly didn't now. He was too good-hearted and sincere for her, too sweet and artless. He was too honorable and too deserving of better than to be stuck with a useless ninny like her.

As tempting—*sorely* tempting—as it was to grab for this lifeline and let him think she might change her mind about accepting his marriage proposal, Stacey realized she hadn't sunk quite low enough to do that to him. She couldn't use an honestly decent man like him to save her own skin. She'd be the lowest of the low if she did that. Particularly now, when she had even less to offer him in return.

"Oh, Oren, I'm s-sor…" The room had taken a hard turn that time. Her choked, "Not feeling we-ell," was little more than a jerky whisper, but he heard it as if she'd spoken in his ear.

The room continued to spin dangerously and she

found herself clinging to him and pressed against his side as he led her along the edge of the crowd. Her knees barely held her up, but his strong hand at her waist kept her anchored safely to him, so no one paid much attention. At least, she didn't think they had.

They'd just reached the relative quiet of the foyer when he stopped. "Are you gonna be sick?"

It took her several moments to decide, but her belated, "No," was belated enough that he'd already ushered her into the private elevator by the time she got it out.

The moment the doors closed, he had her in his arms. He spared a moment to take her tiny evening bag off her wrist and tuck it in his cummerbund, but then his arms went back around her and she was pressed comfortably against him.

"Am I gonna have to carry you, or can you make it to a cab?"

Stacey leaned her cheek against his hard, warm chest because her eyelids were amazingly heavy. She was distantly aware when the elevator stopped, and that she remained on her feet only because he turned so she could cling to his waist. He held her up enough to foster the illusion that she was able to walk under her own power.

She wasn't particularly drunk but she was dizzy and sleepy and slow, yet even so, she didn't want to be carried out. She didn't want everyone's last sight of Stacey Amhearst to be of her being carried out of a building because she'd had too much to drink. It was bad enough that they'd find out in a few more days that she was almost penniless.

At least leaving the party with a tall, rugged stranger would be a plus in their eyes. Until they found out where he was from and what he did for a living.

The warm city night cleared her head a little. McClain led her along the row of cabs waiting at the curb. She was becoming steadier with each step, but when they reached the cab at the head of the line, they walked on past.

Stacey searched ahead for some other cab he must have been aiming for, but there were no other vehicles in the line, so then she looked for a limousine. After several more steps it dawned on her that there were no limos ahead either. She slowed, perplexed.

"Where are we going?"

"The walk'll be good for you," he said, and she glanced up at him, dismayed.

"But it's six blocks. And it must be after midnight."

"It's a nice night."

His naiveté was a shock. "We could be mugged."

Now he smiled a little, blatant evidence that he was far too macho to give a thought to the perils of big city crime. And maybe he was right. McClain was a big man, and he looked rugged and harsh, the quintessential tough-guy, even in an elegant tuxedo. And there was a "don't mess with me" aura about him that most muggers would choose to pass up. There were easier targets.

"But it's six blocks," she reminded him, then felt heat flash into her cheeks. She'd sounded whiney and a little put upon, and she had just enough sense left to be a little ashamed of that in front of a man like him.

It's what she would have said to anyone else and not thought a thing about it, but she'd said it to Oren McClain. A man whose fit, work-hardened body would see a paltry six blocks as laughably light exercise.

"You outta walk off some of that wine," he said gruffly. She heard the hint of disapproval and was embarrassed that she'd been drinking like a fish. He'd caught her at a bad time, and what pride had survived everything else was under sound assault.

"Maybe you're right," she said, then submitted as he again slid his arm around her waist. Her arm went hesitantly around his, and they started. Hopefully, the effects of the wine would numb a little of the ache of walking six blocks on concrete in her heels.

They'd only gone two blocks before her head cleared more and her feet began to hurt enough that she reconsidered her pride in favor of trying to hail a taxi. But because she wanted to behave well while McClain was still around to witness it, she refrained from complaining. Or begging.

By the time they reached her building, got past security and took the swift silent elevator to her apartment, Stacey was abysmally clearheaded, and was already vowing to never again use alcohol to escape her problems. All it had done was make them worse, though something told her that her notion of worse was about to be revised downward.

That little inkling seemed downright prophetic by the time they reached her door and she tried to tell Oren McClain good-night.

"I'd like to see you inside," he said. "Make sure you're all right."

The genuineness in his tone told her he wasn't angling for more than that, though she couldn't actually be sure. He'd been completely trustworthy before, but people were rarely what they seemed on short acquaintance.

And, it was kinder to him to stop things before she gave him any false hopes. Not that she assumed that every man who came in range was instantly lovesick, but because she couldn't overlook that he'd said he was here to see if she'd changed her mind about him. He'd have to be more than a little smitten to do that.

Besides, she didn't want to give herself the opportunity to grab whatever rescue he could provide. It would be wrong to use him, and she wasn't sure how long she could be noble if she spent even a few more minutes with him. And it was a disturbing fact that her body was still reacting to the masculine pull of his, and she still tingled everywhere they'd touched on the walk home.

She made herself say, "I'm all right. Really. I'm just tired now…and embarrassed that I made a fool of myself."

One side of his stern mouth curved slightly. "You didn't make a fool of yourself, Miss Stacey. You're the same proper lady you always are. Just a little thirsty."

Stacey so liked the gently scolding tone in his gravely voice—as if he thought she was too hard on herself—but his kind words hurt. He was so gallant.

Too gallant to string along or exploit.

"Thank you," she said quietly. "Good night, Mr. McClain." She turned toward the door.

"You might need this," he said, and she glanced back. Seeing the tiny handbag, she took it, fumbled with the catch, then got out her key. Her hand was steady enough to unlock the door.

She felt her body tingle again as he reached past her to push open the door, so she stepped quickly inside and turned.

"I'd like to see you tomorrow," he said. "Take you to lunch somewhere."

Stacey knew he meant to try to court her again, and she couldn't allow that. It took almost more will than she had to tell him so.

"I'm...sorry. I'm truly sorry, Oren. It wouldn't be...right." She almost bit her lip again for calling him Oren. Using his first name after she'd called him Mr. McClain seemed far too personal, and maybe even a little inviting.

As if he hadn't noticed anything but her refusal, a stoniness came over him. Had she hurt his feelings or merely made him angry?

Though he couldn't know she no longer had a house staff, she was very aware that they were the only two people here. If he was a threat to her at all, she might be in trouble more serious than losing her fortune.

She was afraid of him—he was so big and tough that he could hurt her with very little effort—and yet she wasn't afraid of him at all. He might not pass muster with the etiquette police, or know which fork to use, or how to properly greet royalty and important guests in a receiving line, but he was a complete gentleman.

"All right then, Miss Stacey," he said, and his rugged face seemed merely solemn. He lifted his hand to an inside pocket and withdrew a business card. He held it out to her.

"I wrote the name of my hotel there, and the room number. I'm stayin' till Thursday. After Thursday, you can get hold of me at any of those numbers."

Stacey made herself take the card because he didn't deserve rudeness, and he was perceptive enough not to need a strong rebuff. Proof of that was when he turned and crossed the short distance to the elevator.

Stacey literally had to press her fingers over her lips to keep from calling him back. She managed to step farther into her apartment to let her door go shut before he could get into the elevator and turn so she could see his face. Stacey listened to the latch on her door catch securely, then heard the elevator doors close.

Had she just done Oren McClain a kindness, or had she just cut off her last chance for an easy rescue?

CHAPTER TWO

THERE was nothing noble about the ghostly pale face in the mirror late that next morning or the self-pitying thoughts she was wallowing in. Stacey forced herself through the motions of a hot shower and the numbing discipline of doing her makeup and hair before she wandered into one of her closets to decide what to wear for the day.

The almost military precision of the spacing between the hangers of clothes on one side of the huge closet mocked her. Angelique had taken meticulous care of her clothes, hanging them just so and stuffing them here and there with rumpled tissue paper to prevent wrinkling. Every shoe and boot had been placed with equal precision in their slots according to color in one of the sections, and Stacey knew her underthings were laid away with the same obsessive neatness and attention to color that had made Angelique a neurotic's dream.

But the simple fact was that in less than a week Stacey had already proven a failure at maintaining the rigid order that had come so effortlessly to her maid. The left side of the closet was a mess, with wads of tissue here and there on the carpet. Her

inability to maintain order, like her every other little incompetence over trivial things, had further
undermined Stacey's secret lack of self-confidence
and left her feeling increasingly inept and adrift.

Though she'd been raised by an elderly grandfather who'd seen women as social ornaments
whose chief aims should be to marry well and be
an asset to a wealthy husband, there was really no
excuse in this day and age to not have pursued
some kind of career that could at least support her.

But the truth was, she'd been petted and cos-
seted and spoiled until she was fairly useless. Yes,
she'd filled up her time with charities and social
activities and a political cause or two, but not much
of that could be converted into the kind of cold
cash that might keep her in her wealthy lifestyle
of ease.

She really would make a good wife to some
hard-driven millionaire who was looking for a trophy with a pedigreed background, but she'd be a
zero at going it alone. Anything in life that hadn't
come easy or she'd not enjoyed, she'd been free
to walk away from. And had.

But there was no walking away from the fact
that in a few days, most of her beautiful things
would be hauled off to storage in a warehouse
somewhere, and she'd be living in a less exclusive
section of the city. She'd be learning how to make

her way around on buses and subways while she continued to search for a job she could do that would pay enough to keep a roof over her head. It would also have to pay the storage bill until she could bear to part with her things.

If she'd taken over her own finances three years ago when her grandfather had passed away instead of blithely continuing with the latent crook who'd slowly embezzled her money to invest in several risky financial schemes, she wouldn't be in this mess.

Her only hope was that investigators could locate both him and what might be left of her money, and somehow get it back. The thief had fled to South America somewhere, so the hunt was not only complicated by distance but by the difficulties of cooperation between law enforcement agencies that often had more pressing crimes to solve than embezzled funds.

Her brain made another edgy circuit around every problem and frustration, and when it had replayed each one, a mental review of possible catastrophes began their inevitable parade through her thoughts. Her head had been pounding before she'd gotten out of bed that morning just after eleven, but even after a hefty dose of aspirin, it continued to thump. Whether the thumping was solely from the headache or merely the punishment of tortured thoughts, the pain was the same, as was the queasy anxiety she felt.

When she'd finally chosen something to put on and got dressed, Stacey walked out into her bedroom. Her gaze fell to the ivory carpet and fixed on the business card McClain had given her. She thought she'd tossed it in the wastebasket but she must have missed, and it had ended up on the floor.

The sight of it was a profound irritation. She couldn't even throw something away and do it successfully. Aggravated, she picked up the card and started to toss it away again before she suddenly froze.

The bold scrawl on the back of the card gave the name of one of the most beautiful and exclusive hotels in New York. Seeing how he'd written the letters gave her a swift sense of McClain himself: bold, masculine, decisive.

His handwriting wasn't something spidery or refined-looking or difficult to read. It was as blunt as he was, as unpretentious, but the letters seemed confident. The pressure he'd put on the pen fairly shouted guilessness; he'd not needed to dither over what to write, he'd just done it. He was a man who said what he meant and meant what he said, and there'd be no mistaking him because he was too straightforward.

Holding that card in her fingers seemed to calm

a little of the anxiety that made her feel so sick. No one would cheat or steal from a man like McClain, if for no other reason than the fact that he looked like he could beat the daylights out of anyone foolish enough to trifle with him.

If he were in her place, he certainly wouldn't be moping around his house wondering how he'd survive or where he'd live. He probably wouldn't care that his closets weren't tidy or feel incompetent because he couldn't cook for himself or do his own laundry.

He wouldn't be afraid to look for a job. If his friends shunned him, he'd probably say ''To hell with them,'' and he'd put all his energy and strength into making his own way in the world, even if he'd need to find some new way to live.

That was her impression of Oren McClain. Because of that, she wondered again what a man like him could possibly see in someone like her. Or was he the kind of man her archaic and chauvinistic grandfather had raised her to marry? The kind of man so driven and taken up with his wealth or position or his business life that he'd choose a wife as an accessory and make certain he selected one with breeding who could provide him with handsome and/or beautiful heirs?

Stacey supposed some Texas ranchers and oil-men might be the same on that score as some of the moneyed eastern elites. She turned the card over and read down through the list of phone numbers. There were six of those.

She felt a spark of hope. If Oren McClain was looking for a trophy wife, he might not be disappointed in her. She took good care of her skin and her body, and she had personal taste and a refined style that would never be an embarrassment to him.

Surely he wasn't looking for a woman who could outride, outrope and outcowboy him, because he could have found a woman like that in Texas. Before her hope could rise very far, Stacey got a swift mental picture of a Texas cattle ranch. How did anyone survive socially and culturally so far from a city?

Did McClain have a maid? A cook? He'd talked like he had money, but how much money did he actually have? And how did he spend it? Did he spend it all on cows and land and pickup trucks and cowboy hobbies, or would he spend some on household help? How big was his house? Was it a cabin or something with some real size to it?

She thought again of his remark about jewels and designer duds. Her impression of him was of honesty and straightforwardness. Maybe he hadn't exaggerated the things he could provide a wife. If anything, McClain might be the kind of man who understated things to avoid appearing a braggart.

Stacey's hopes rose a little more as she considered all that. He'd said he'd come to New York to see her, to find out if she'd changed her mind, but she couldn't just take him at face value. She needed more information, but she needed a means to get it that wouldn't cost very much.

An Internet search got her started. Going by McClain's business card, she found out which part of Texas he was from and managed to find newspaper coverage that mentioned McClain Ranch and McClain Oil. A social page in a San Antonio newspaper mentioned an Oren McClain in an article about an area fund-raiser weeks ago, but something else that had gotten her attention was the fact that a TV Western mini-series had been shot on location on McClain Ranch.

Stacey began to feel a little more at ease about Oren McClain. He apparently wasn't a social outcast, he was well known in the area of Texas he was from, and she hadn't seen his name associated with anything criminal.

She gave a self-deprecating groan. Her grandfather would have had the background of any potential husband investigated at least as far back as three generations, and he would have had to know to the penny how much the man was worth. Stacey was reduced to doing an Internet search to rule out a criminal background and reading through a so-

ciety page and business directory to see if the man
had enough resources to support a spoiled wife.

Disgusted that she'd gone this far toward the
idea of marrying a stranger for his money, she got
up and started to pace. Though her apartment was
large it seemed to grow more oppressively small
by the hour.

She thought about the money she'd had over the
years. Or rather, the money she'd spent. What
she'd give for a year's worth of the money she'd
spent on clothing and jewelry alone! And now she
couldn't buy much of anything. What little she had
left would have to fund a new, painfully modest
life. And what if she couldn't find a job? She'd
already waited two months for something she
could live with.

The grim future she pictured for herself made it
nearly impossible to contemplate the wait between
now and Monday, when she could again call the
employment agency she'd consulted in hopes of
finding something she was qualified to do.

Saturday night loomed before her like lonely
shadows in a long dark hall. She was already sick
of the deli food in the refrigerator. A fine, hot meal
would go a long way in calming her jitters and
helping her shore up what little actual courage she
had.

Stacey glanced over at the business card propped

up on the computer keyboard and realized she was in serious danger of sinking low enough to take advantage of Oren McClain.

Perhaps it wouldn't be so awful to at least find out if he'd like to take her to dinner. Maybe he wasn't really serious about marriage. After all, he said he'd come to New York to see if her answer was still no. Perhaps if he took her out once or twice, he'd realize that he didn't really want her to say yes. She might be doing him a favor if she let him spend enough time with her to become disillusioned.

Stacey didn't let herself think about how far she'd twisted things around to make her selfish motives—and her craving for a hot meal—seem noble. Not until she'd made the call to McClain's hotel and let him know she'd changed her mind about seeing him.

Once they'd made plans for the evening and she'd hung up the phone, she felt so heartsick over her cowardly scheme that she almost, *almost* called him back.

The lady was as jumpy as a flea on an old dog. He could almost smell her guilt over their date tonight, and he was satisfied by that hint of character.

A little aristocrat like Stacey Amhearst was probably terrified of being poor, and she was no doubt close to the point where she'd do just about anything to save herself from the horrors of being broke. She might even marry a rough old Texas boy like him.

She'd secretly studied him all through dinner as if she was judging a horse she might buy. He knew she liked the way he made her feel because he couldn't mistake the way she'd melted when he'd escorted her across the restaurant with his hand at the back of her waist.

Or earlier, when he'd picked her up at her place and taken her arm to go downstairs to get in the taxi. And again when they'd arrived here and he'd taken her hand for the short walk from the taxi into the restaurant.

The lady was like a choice sweet in a kid's warm grip, and he liked that her cool grace and polite reserve was about as thin as a cellophane wrapper. Months ago, she'd behaved as if she hadn't quite known how to handle him—or herself—when he got close. She still behaved that way, but he couldn't tell if that was because she liked him more than she wanted to or if she just didn't have much experience with men like him. At least she seemed to enjoy being with him.

He probably came off like a brute compared to the men she was used to. Hell, he was no peacock. His skin had been burned brown by the sun and weathered by the elements, his hands were big and scarred and thick with calluses, and the only truly fragile and refined thing in his life was her.

But she might marry him anyway, because he had money and she knew he wanted her. She'd be torn up with guilt over it because she'd be marrying him for something other than love. How he knew that was more because of what he'd sensed about her than any bit of gossip he'd been able to ferret out.

Though he could be wrong, his instincts were usually on target. They told him Ms. Stacey Amhearst knew right from wrong. She just didn't have enough confidence in herself—yet—to do right and damn the consequences. He meant to benefit from that while he could.

Oren leaned back to watch as she picked up her last spoon and dug into dessert. Though he knew from months ago that she'd been raised to pick and fuss daintily over her food, she'd gone after her meal tonight like a half-starved cattle crew at a cookhouse table.

The reason was obvious. She'd lost weight she couldn't spare, and that was because she couldn't do for herself in the kitchen. How the hell her grandfather could have raised her to be so helpless was a marvel to Oren McClain. No daughter of his would be dependent on anyone.

No wife of his would either. His only real criticism of Stacey was that she'd stayed helpless and dependent, though he meant to see that change. There was no reason in the world that she couldn't have class and beauty and grace along with a hefty dose of can-do independence and the self-confidence that went with it.

"So tell me, Oren," she began after she'd mostly finished the artsy dab that passed for a big city dessert. He enjoyed the sound of his name when she said it. She made it sound dignified and upper crust. "About your ranch. Is it just outside San Antonio?"

Oren smiled. "It's about three hours outside, give or take." He noticed she picked up her cloth napkin and touched it to her lips as if to think about that. Or to cover a rush of dismay.

"What do you do so far out? For entertainment."

"We've got dances, church socials, barbecues, rodeos, school events. There's a county fair and an occasional parade. Several small town celebrations and events, a couple honky-tonks for nightlife and weekends, a golf course, a lake, and we have our own doings at the ranch. Buyers and business folks fly in. I sometimes drive out or fly out to other places when something interests me or work takes me away."

SUSAN FOX · 37

He could tell she was mentally trying to picture
all that—and whether she could tolerate it or not—
so he added, ''Most folks in town or on the land
are good people, lots are family folk and real
friendly. Salt of the earth.''

The down-home, plain-folk descriptions must
have rattled her a little because she made a big
production of returning her napkin to her lap and
then kept looking down as she fiddled with it.
When she finally looked up, the smile she gave
him looked a little too strained to be as serene as
she must have meant.

''They sound...very nice,'' she said, then
reached for her water glass and took a delicate sip
that made him stare at the way her lips handled
the task.

As if catching him staring at her mouth unsettled
her, she quickly put down the glass and offered
him a self-conscious smile. She casually pushed
her dessert plate a little away, and he guessed she
was finished with it.

Oren lazily returned her smile. ''How do I get
the waiter to bring me the check so we can get out
of this place?''

He was as much as declaring to her that he was
a country hick, and as he'd hoped, she took it
kindly. Now she smiled a little less tensely.

She lifted her napkin to the table and laid it

neatly beside her plate, and her voice was low enough to not be overheard.

"They're very good with subtleties here. You might try doing this." She discretely lifted a slender index finger then immediately put it down.

McClain grinned over at her and Stacey watched as he glanced away and went solemn. The momentary glitter that flashed in his dark eyes was as effective as a shout and immediately their waiter was at his side with a small silver tray.

McClain tossed a couple large denomination bills on the tray with a low, "Keep it," that made the waiter murmur his thanks and vanish as quickly as he'd appeared.

Stacey realized she hadn't seen McClain take out his wallet, and she wondered how long he'd been waiting for her to finish dessert. He'd declined one for himself, but she'd been too impolite to deny herself when he'd encouraged her to choose a dessert. Or rather, she'd been too selfish and greedy to pass up what was surely a last opportunity for a decadent treat.

Now he winked at her. "You're right about these folks. They understand subtle."

And then he stood up, and it wasn't necessarily her imagination that his size and his masculine presence caused the murmurs at the tables nearby to pause a moment, as if a giant had suddenly stood up among them. Oren came around to her side of the table and casually pulled her chair back for her to rise.

And then he took her elbow with hard, strong fingers that were absolutely gentle and almost scorchingly hot. And magical.

Never had she felt the things Oren McClain made her feel. Every time he touched her, the tiny shocks and shivery tingles he set off rapidly gathered in places she'd not known could feel things like that.

It was part of what had overwhelmed her about him before. Every time he'd touched her and she'd felt like this, she'd gotten the very strong sense that if he ever did more than touch her a little or kiss her, she'd lose control of herself and somehow be lost. For someone who'd kept herself remote from all but a friend's casual touch or occasional hug, the whole issue of physical intimacy was unknown territory.

Or maybe it was because Oren McClain was such a physical man with such a virile presence. A reserved woman like her had little enough experience, but with a man like him it was difficult to know what to expect when it came to delicate sexual matters.

She, of course, knew all about the mechanics of sex, but knowledge was worlds away from actual experience. And instinct warned that even if she'd had a bit of experience with sex, an intimate encounter Oren McClain would be completely unique. He was too elemental, too completely male, and too supremely confident in himself not to be dynamic and possibly quite primitive in bed.

Why had a man like him chosen her? Did he want a meek woman to dominate? He was a man who could naturally dominate anyone, including most men, but she sensed that was purely accidental because of his size and rugged looks. He'd been anything but overbearing when she'd been around him.

But then, he didn't need to be. As with the waiter who'd responded to a mere gleam in a single, momentary look, McClain needed to do little more than show an inkling of his will to get his way.

Stacey thought about that as they stepped out of the restaurant and paused under the canopy at the end of the walk to wait for a taxi. The night was warmer tonight than it had been last night. Then again, heat was pouring off McClain and Stacey felt flushed with nerves and uncertainty.

And she had the absurd impulse to cry. She'd let herself down in so many ways that she couldn't begin to keep track of them all. She was ashamed of being afraid to stand on her own two feet, but shame wasn't enough to prompt her to overcome her fears. Not even the worry that she might grab the easy rescue McClain seemed to offer and unintentionally jump from the frying pan into the fire, was enough to put some starch in her spine.

She never should have come to this; she'd never in her life dreamed of coming to this. But here she was, after months of growing impotence as she'd made one shocking discovery after another, then had failed, time after time, to catch up with the thief or to prevent a single disaster.

The rarified life her grandfather had died believing he'd safeguarded for her was nearly gone, except for the trust fund she'd have at age thirty. Not only was her access to it six years away, but she didn't truly believe it wouldn't somehow disappear like all the rest, stolen by a financial sleight of hand by some other larcenous predator.

And considering her financial circumstances, six years might as well be twenty for all the good the trust fund would do her now. Her grandfather's attorney had been so "sincerely regretful," but there was nothing he could do.

As McClain opened a cab door and gently ushered her in, Stacey managed a brief smile of thanks. He slid in beside her and lifted his arm to rest it on the seat behind her, effectively distracting her from her unhappy thoughts.

Though he didn't actually touch her anywhere, the heat from his big body seared her from shoulder to ankle, and she couldn't seem to keep from melting a little. It took quite a lot to keep from leaning into the heat of him.

Why was it so natural to want to press close to him? This couldn't be love, because love was a far more tender and delicate emotion. Wasn't it? Love surely couldn't be this craving for the feel of a hard, masculine body or the gentle touch of a callus-rough hand. A craving that had little or nothing to do with high-minded and hazy romantic sentiment but yet everything to do with bodily urges and lust.

Yes, that was it: lust. Something that could be powerfully and potently felt, but something too volatile and flesh-driven not to burn up quickly. Love was something pure and tender and sweet, something that occurred in the mind and in the heart, and endured.

Lust was primitive and indiscriminate, and involved only baser sensibilities. Lust was all around, but it certainly didn't make for a better society, and it certainly was nothing to base a marriage on.

And neither was the desperate need for money. Stacey folded her hands together in her lap and resisted the impulse to introduce some harmless bit of conversation to help pass the time on the ride home. It was better that Oren McClain realized now how little they had in common.

Since many men relied on their women to take care of the social niceties of polite conversation, dropping the burden in his lap might make him realize that a little sooner and he'd lose interest.

There were better women in the world who were more suited to him and his rural way of life, and it would be a shame if he wasted any more time or thought on a frivolous ninny like her.

CHAPTER THREE

THEY rode the elevator in continued silence. It was almost as if the tension between them was building with each floor they passed until, all too soon, they'd reached her floor and were stepping out.

There'd be no stiffly polite "Good night, Mr. McClain," at the door tonight. Something had happened in the cab on the ride back from supper, and Stacey couldn't discern exactly what it was or how she'd known it. All she was sure of was that she'd sensed that a decision had been made, and that her companion had pledged himself to it.

Clinging to her poise, she unlocked her door and led the way into the large apartment. It seemed even more silent and tense here, as if her secrets were lurking, keeping still to avoid discovery and yet just as apt to suddenly spring out of hiding.

Of course, there was nothing lurking behind anything. Instead, it was her conscience that was nettling her and making itself sharply felt. And it needed to nettle her because cowardice was having a heyday, and she was all but crossing her fingers in the hope that Oren McClain would repeat his marriage proposal tonight.

Because she'd also made a decision in the taxi: to accept his proposal. But then they'd walked into her building and she'd decided to turn him down. When they'd reached her floor, she'd reversed her decision again and decided to marry him.

She'd have to keep her desperate financial troubles from him but she had enough money left to keep the true state of her situation a secret, at least for a time. And yet, wasn't it wrong to hide the truth?

Secrets, particularly enormous ones like hers, couldn't make for a successful marriage. A surreptitious glance at the big man told her she'd be an idiot to cross him. If he was unhappy with her, or she disappointed him too much, they'd have zero chance at anything livable together.

Though he was open and uncomplicated and straightforward, that didn't necessarily translate to being long-suffering or self-sacrificing or easygoing. He'd have expectations of her. Big ones. But what would they be exactly?

Common sense told her that she'd disappointed herself too much not to also disappoint him. And marrying a man so different from her, particularly this soon, was asking for trouble. She'd had too much failure and trouble lately to risk landing herself in more, though at the moment she couldn't think of anything worse than facing what she would by the end of the week. Or what would come after that.

Spending the evening with a rugged, self-assured man who was so gallant and solicitous of her had provided a feeling of safety and security that was almost as irresistible as his touches were. That was why it was hard to cling to the notion of associating serious trouble with the idea of marrying McClain.

And it was a fact that McClain was the only man to ever affect her the way he had. Didn't that count for something in all this?

Once they reached her spacious living room, Stacey invited him to sit down. He chose the sofa, and it amazed her how much his size seemed to dwarf it.

"Would you like something to drink?" she asked. At least she had a variety of beverages. And she did know how to brew coffee.

"Just talk for me, thanks."

He was so straightforward, and Stacey felt the tension between them go a few notches higher. The look on his rugged face was stern, and she couldn't miss his solemnity. Just like before when he'd proposed.

Stacey quailed a little inside. She wasn't prepared for this, not really. She wasn't sure what to say or how to say it. She wasn't sure about anything, and she suddenly realized she didn't want the responsibility of making any permanent choices.

Mostly because she was terrified of the consequences, either way. If she told him no this time, she knew there'd never be a third chance. But if she said yes, could she live up to the expectations of a man who lived in the wilds of Texas? A man she didn't know well outside of a handful of days, several months ago, and what little she'd found out about him on the Internet today?

McClain put out a big hand and the faint lift of one corner of his mouth coaxed her to come close. She stepped hesitantly around the large crystal coffee table and forced herself to place her cold fingers in range of his hard grip.

His hand closed warmly around hers and Stacey obediently perched on the edge of the sofa cushion next to him. Her senses were so raw and alive that she felt brittle and wary.

To cover it, she rushed out with an awkward, ''Thank you for tonight.''

McClain's black gaze was intent on hers, and she felt as if he was probing her brain. She couldn't control the guilty heat that climbed into her cheeks. He didn't waste time with small talk.

"You know what I want to ask, Miss Stacey."

Her nerves jumped at the low words, and her gaze fled the somber gleam in his. She wanted to get this over with, and yet she didn't want it to happen at all. If he didn't propose tonight, she wouldn't have to decide anything. Delay was the only thing she could think of.

"You seem...in a hurry."

She couldn't help looking at him again to see how he'd taken that. The solemnity about him was a confirmation that there'd be no delay, particularly when he spoke.

"Life's short. I see what I want."

The suddenness of this still mystified her. She'd heard about love at first sight, but she didn't believe in it. And then it occurred to her that they might not be talking about the same thing. Perhaps all he wanted now was an affair. It shamed her a little to realize that she'd automatically expected him to propose marriage again. Perhaps that hadn't been his intent at all, particularly after she'd turned him down once before.

"Then you aren't looking for a...long-term relationship.'' And even if he did mean marriage, he might not be talking about the till-death-do-us-part kind.

There was absolutely no flicker of change on his rugged face, but his voice went lower and rougher.

''Only about as long term as fifty or sixty years. If we're lucky.''

Stacey stared at him, searching his expression for some clue to all this. Had it been love at first sight for him? Did that happen to tough macho types? And even if it did, she'd never believe it amounted to anything more than lust. He hadn't known her very well at all and he still didn't, so his heart couldn't possibly be involved.

Her heart certainly wasn't. Yes, he'd got her attention, yes he thrilled her, and double-yes, he was a potential rescuer, but she felt little more than a level of fondness for him. He was a man almost completely out of her experience, with interests that were surely so different from hers that they couldn't possibly mesh.

Because she'd hoped to one day fall in love and somehow defy the kind of sterile marriages that were based on money and breeding and the outwardly stiff, ho-hum affection that so many of her peers' marriages seemed to be based on, she had to ask what she did next. She was also probing for a clue to McClain's thinking.

"What about love, Mr. McClain? Isn't that the most important consideration when two people make a commitment to a relationship that will span fifty or sixty years?"

Now she caught the frank cynicism in his dark eyes and got her first inkling that McClain was anything but uncomplicated.

"Look around, Miss Stacey. Lots of folks fall in love, but they just as easily fall out. I'm willing to bet on natural chemistry and deliberate choice. We've got the chemistry. All that's left is the choice."

Now he reached into his inside jacket pocket with his free hand and Stacey saw the small flash when he brought it back out. There, circling the tip of his index finger was a simple solitaire diamond on a gold engagement band.

"I choose you, you choose me."

Stacey couldn't keep from staring at the ring. It was simple, but elegant, and she was experienced enough with fine jewelry to know it cost a fortune. McClain not only made sudden, stunning decisions, he also backed them to the hilt. Was that a sign of arrogance, or confidence? Or both?

And was she reassured by this or horrified? She

made herself look up from the ring to his waiting gaze.

"My goodness," she said, suddenly aware how
long she'd kept him waiting while she'd ogled the
diamond and tried to read it like a crystal ball.
"You seem…determined."

And breathtakingly sure of me.

"Maybe." His one-word reply made her search
his somber expression. "Like I said, I came back
to see if things had changed for you. If they
haven't, we'll part friends."

Yes, but I'll never see you again, her heart impulsively added, and she was taken aback by the
way that felt. The thought of never seeing McClain
again caused a sad little ache.

And though he'd made the consequences of a
second refusal sound harmless, she sensed he'd
done that because his pride had stooped low
enough when he'd decided to come here again. As
she'd already known, there'd be no third chance,
but she liked that he wouldn't declare it in so many
words. That was probably also because of his
pride, but she appreciated being spared the extra
pressure.

At least, the extra pressure from him. Inside, she
felt an almost crushing pressure as her brain again
reviewed what was at stake: She was in desperate

financial straits…she suddenly didn't want to close the door between them forever…she somehow knew that whatever McClain's expectations of her were, he at least wanted her enough now to be distracted from any wifely incompetencies. At least for a while.

After all, it wasn't as if she'd be cooking for him or doing his laundry or cleaning his house. He *had* to realize she couldn't do any of those sorts of things, and he surely wouldn't expect her to. She could be a companion to him, have his children, run his household and entertain his guests.

In return, she'd have a chance at the family she'd secretly dreamed of, and she'd never have to worry about money again. Even if he turned out to not be filthy rich, he at least had a home and a substantial income. And as long as they were together, she'd never have to face trouble alone.

Unless Oren McClain proved to be more trouble than she already had.

She'd hesitated almost too long. She realized it when she felt the restless brush of his thumb against the back of her hand and she sensed the fresh pull of tension in his big body.

Her soft, ''Oh,'' made the glitter in his dark eyes flare the tiniest bit. ''Oh, ah…Oren. Are you certain I'm the right woman for you? I don't know anything about cows or ranches. I've hardly even driven my car." He replied instantly to that.

"I pay folks to do for me, Miss Stacey. What I don't have is a wife. Or babies," he added gruffly, then stared into her eyes the longest moment.

She got the impression that he was some kind of human polygraph, and that he'd instantly know it if she lied. And the way he was looking at her now made her wonder if he'd already sensed something amiss. He went on somberly.

"If you don't want to carry kids and help me raise them, I'd appreciate knowing straight-out."

He was so grim when he'd said that. The issue of bearing his children and sharing the task of raising them was deadly serious to him. Nonnegotiable. She liked him for that, liked him enormously. She'd suffered a lot by not having two parents for most of her childhood, and she certainly wanted more for her own children than life had allotted her.

"I do want children," she said. "But what if things don't... work between us?"

"Then we'll be no worse off than the folks who thought they were in love."

Stacey looked down at the big hand that had virtually swallowed hers up. She should tell McClain about her lost fortune, but how would he react if he knew she was on the verge of saying yes because she was desperate for money?

Would it hurt his feelings to find that out? Would he think less of her? She did like him, and had from the moment they'd met. She just didn't love him, and her desperate situation made it impossible to think of much more than the financial lifeline he represented.

And honestly, it was a fact that she would have told him no right away last night if she hadn't been in such a horrible fix.

He'd surely think less of her once he knew what had happened. A man like him would have no respect for a spoiled little airhead who'd left herself open to being taken advantage of and robbed, particularly when it had been her own laziness and selfish distraction that had put her in that position.

"M-maybe I should…confide a few things."

The words had just popped out, and she felt the panicked compulsion to call them back. She couldn't, of course. And she should have known she couldn't have lived with keeping the truth from him.

Though Oren McClain was big and tough and macho, and he looked impervious to hurt feelings, he was human. Whatever his reaction might be now, if she didn't tell him the truth, he'd be hurt when he found out later.

She'd not wanted some fortune hunter to heartlessly target her for what he could get, so it made sense that McClain wouldn't want that either. It might even have been part of why he'd been so attracted to her months ago. Because she'd been rich, he wouldn't have needed to wonder whether she was responding to him for himself or only for his money.

The silence stretched. He hadn't made a verbal reply or comment on what she'd just said about confiding a few things, but she sensed he was waiting alertly for her to go on. Emotion welled up and she did her very best to not show it or let it affect her voice because she couldn't stand for him to pity her any more than she could bear his scorn. It wasn't easy to make her voice sound matter-of-fact, but she managed it.

"I can't marry you, Oren. It wouldn't be fair to you." She pulled her hand from his, grateful when he allowed it to slip free. She stood to her feet and turned to walk back around the crystal coffee table.

His drawled, "How so?" pursued her. She stopped and gripped her hands together, reluctant to face him. She was too cowardly to look him in the eye and actually see his first reaction.

It felt as if everything in the universe had suddenly come to attention and turned to bear down on her. The actual words were difficult to get out.

"I'm...almost broke," she confessed, her voice going small and soft with the effort not to sound teary. She tried to get in a breath, then made herself look over at him calmly. "It's not fair to take advantage of you. Marrying you might solve all my problems, but yours will multiply."

His face went stony and any sense of vulnerability she'd sensed in him—or hoped for—evaporated. He was so still and when he kept silent for several more moments, she went on.

"If I said yes to you now, you'd never really be sure of my affection for you, whether it was honest or not, or whether it was only your money that I loved." She gave a humorless smile. "After all, when I had money I liked you a lot, but I still said no. I can't accept a second chance under these circumstances."

His dark gaze narrowed. "Do you still like me?"

Stacey stared a moment, caught off guard. Surely that couldn't make a difference to him.

"You deserve a woman who falls in love with you before she gets your ring on her finger. A woman who wouldn't care whether you had money or not. I'm not that woman, Oren. Not really.''

Her voice hitched on that last, and she felt a tide of heat rise up her throat and singe her cheeks. It wasn't from embarrassment, but rather from the wild surge of emotions that stormed through her because she'd deliberately sacrificed her last chance of an easy rescue in favor of doing the right thing by McClain.

Or rather, the right thing by *Oren*. His first name was old-fashioned and naive-sounding. The kind of name that suggested the person called by it was too honest and good-hearted to expect guile and deceit from others. The kind of person who could be swindled out of something precious to them because their motives were too pure to see evil in the motives of less honorable people.

Though the reality was that Oren McClain seemed anything but naive, she sensed he might be vulnerable somehow. Whether he was or he wasn't, she couldn't be the one to take advantage of him or to use him for her own selfish reasons. If she came out of this with nothing else, at least she could comfort herself with the knowledge that she'd done the right thing this time.

Some of her tension eased a little as she watched him lift his hand and slip the beautiful ring back inside the breast pocket of his fine suit. The evening would swiftly come to an end now. He'd walk out and she'd never see him again.

Now that it was over, her knees suddenly felt too shaky and weak to hold her up, so she moved toward one of the armchairs. McClain rose smoothly to his feet and in little more than a normal step for him, he intercepted her.

The jolt she felt when he gently caught her hand almost finished her shaky knees and she turned toward him to brace her free hand against his solid chest. That was all she had time to register before his dark head descended and his hard lips settled possessively on hers.

She was suddenly standing on tiptoe as his strong arms crushed her against him. Her arms automatically went around his neck and she was lost just that quickly beneath the relentless drive of his mouth.

Any kiss they'd had before had been sweet and almost chaste compared to this very carnal mating of lips. It was as if a dam had broken, first in him and then in her. The worry she'd had months ago about being overwhelmed by him was validated as he plied her lips and then moved his big hands over her with a boldness and male expertise that dis-

SUSAN FOX   59

pensed with her will as effortlessly as tossing away
a tissue.

Before she realized it, he was sitting in the armchair with her across his lap and she was clinging
wildly to him. His hands roamed wherever he
wanted, and Stacey was so breathless and taken
over that she was a spineless, shaking heap.

Just when she thought she might lose conscious-
ness, he shifted his lips from hers and held her
tightly against him. Their bodies pulsed together
with the thundering rhythm of hearts that were still
overexcited, and it seemed to take forever before
either one slowed to a more normal rate.

McClain pressed a warm kiss to her forehead
then into her hair before his jaw settled just below
her temple. His breath gusted warmly over her ear.

''You wanna sell your things or ship 'em to
Texas?''

Stacey squeezed her eyes closed. Kissing him
like she had just now was as good as surrender,
and McClain had virtually declared victory.

A sweet little wisp of hope flickered to life. He
knew she was broke, and he still wanted to marry
her. And he knew she didn't love him, but that
didn't matter to him either. What did matter to
Oren McClain?

Stacey lifted her head and tried to reestablish

some sort of distance, though his strong arms allowed her only so much space. She met his gaze, and at such close range she felt a deep connection to him. He lifted a hand to catch a stray lock of hair on her flushed cheek and tenderly nudge it back into place.

"There's something you should know too," he said, his voice low and gravelly. "I heard about your trouble. Figured this was as good a time as any to see you again." His dark gaze dropped to her lips briefly then shifted back up to hers. "Does that bother you?"

Stacey was surprised, and she gave her head an absent shake. "I'm not sure." And she wasn't. Her head was still spinning from the kiss and also with the knowledge that her life was about to change in ways she couldn't completely imagine yet.

"So if anyone's taking advantage, it might be me," he told her.

Stacey warmed toward him a little more. He truly was honest, and she felt the first tendrils of real trust begin between them.

"You didn't somehow arrange for a man who'd worked for my grandfather for ten years to steal my money and leave me like this, did you?" She searched his dark eyes, not truly believing that he'd had anything to do with it, but needing to hear what he would say.

"I might be guilty of catching a lady at a weak moment, but I'm sure as hell not the kind of man who'd ruin one just to get her to marry me."

Oh my, even the idea that she might have thought for a small second that he was capable of doing something that dastardly had obviously offended him. There was no mistaking the flare of temper that had shown in his dark eyes.

Stacey put her palm on his chest in silent apology. "Thank you for telling me." She gave a shaky little smile. "We are such strangers, Oren. It's not a healthy way to start a marriage."

Now a faint smile curved the hard line of his mouth. She sensed his strong self-confidence and envied him for it.

"We'll do fine, Miss Stacey." He reached back into his breast pocket and again took out the ring. "Shall I do the honors?"

Stacey stared at the ring. It looked ridiculously small between his thumb and forefinger, and she felt like the biggest fraud in the world as she made herself nod.

McClain took her left hand. Tenderly, he singled out her ring finger and deftly slipped the beautiful ring into place.

And then he pulled her close and gave her one of the sweetest, most gentle kisses she'd ever had. A small sob of worry and fear threatened to spoil it, but Stacey managed to keep it back until after McClain had left her apartment.

By the time she'd got ready for bed and turned off the lights, she'd almost worn out the rugs pacing. She laid in the dark for a long time, so worried about what she'd agreed to do that she fretted about it half the night. Eventually she convinced herself that marrying McClain might be a radical enough thing to do that it might actually turn out to be one of the best decisions she'd ever made.

She chose to ignore the reminder that she hadn't actually *decided* to marry him that final time. In truth, the decision had just sort of evolved—because she hadn't had the will or the spine to make a strong case to either of them for turning McClain down.

She tried to take comfort in the idea that she hadn't really wanted to turn McClain down. After all, he was still the most exciting man she'd ever met.

And the most overwhelming.

CHAPTER FOUR

McCLAIN was also one of the most efficient people she'd ever met. Like a seasoned general on a battlefield, he commandeered the troops and materiel needed to pack up every single thing she owned and send it on its way to Texas. She'd already made arrangements for the movers to arrive on Monday to begin packing up, but it was McClain who took over and dealt with the moving company on the change in destination. He also took care of canceling her storage arrangements.

He'd taken her for a marriage license first thing on Monday morning, then arranged for a simple ceremony that would take place early on Thursday morning, with a wedding reception brunch that would include her few very close friends just after.

They were on a plane for Texas by one p.m., and landed in San Antonio by late afternoon. Once they'd collected their luggage and transferred it to McClain's Cessna, they flew from San Antonio to arrive at McClain Ranch just after six p.m.

The sight of the ranch headquarters was unexpectedly grand—if you were impressed by trees and barns and buildings, and a massive network of wood-railed and steel-railed corrals that were studded here and there with more trees. Beyond the headquarters, the vast expanse of hills and prairies that stretched miles in every direction looked endless, even from the air.

The house was a sprawling, single-story adobe with a red tile roof that was laid out in a thick C-shape around a shady patio. Unlike a few of the ranches they'd flown over on the way here, there was no pool, but Stacey spied a creek a small distance from the headquarters that widened into a shady spot to create a natural pool before it narrowed again.

The sense of isolation in the vast, almost treeless distances was unsettling to a woman who'd lived her whole life in one of the largest cities in the world. Texas was massive, and McClain Ranch was a big chunk of it.

The farther they'd gone from New York, the more tense and fretful Stacey had become. Only the fact that McClain remained as steady and confident as he'd been all along had given her any sense of security.

And she was preoccupied with a genuine desire not to disappoint him. Not because he'd provided her with a solution to her financial crisis, but because she'd never met anyone in her life who'd done so many good faith things for someone else.

Particularly when he had no real assurance that all the things he was doing for her would be satisfactorily reciprocated.

At one point yesterday, she'd almost thought McClain had changed his mind. Ever since she'd agreed to marry him, he'd been oddly remote. That might have been because he'd given his attention to the movers and the packing and every other little detail he'd thought of before she had, but she'd worried about it anyway. She'd taken care of her own financial business—what there was left of it—including a trip to the police department to check on the progress of her embezzlement case.

McClain had encouraged her to see friends while he'd supervised the movers, so she had, which had left them with even less time together alone. But even then, his touches were cool—though their effect on her wasn't—and any kiss he'd offered had been equally cool and brief.

Almost as if he'd gotten what he wanted and had no real interest in going through the motions of courtship, as he'd done months ago. After all, with the marriage due to happen so quickly, along with the fact that everything she owned was being packed up and sent on its way to Texas in record time, it made sense that McClain had no worries that she'd change her mind.

His increased aloofness yesterday when she'd

moved into his hotel had been impossible to over-look. She'd taken a room just across the hall from his, but he'd not so much as crossed the threshold. At first, she'd taken that as a wordless example of his old-fashioned code of morality, and she'd liked him for it, but even after the ceremony today, he'd been almost rigidly remote.

Which made her feel even more uncertain about him. And uncertain about tonight, since it was their wedding night.

McClain had observed every propriety this week, but she was his wife now and he'd have no reason to keep such a prudent physical distance. On the other hand, she should be relieved. She'd wished all week for separate bedrooms until they got to know each other better, but she was leery of asking for them.

She was deeply, deeply indebted to McClain and, ready or not, she owed him his due as a husband. But what did he think about it? Did he believe he'd bought a wife?

The question made her feel even more as if she'd sold herself. That was partly why she'd insisted on paying for the packers and movers, as well as the costs of shipping her things. It had been important to her to pay her way, including her hotel room, though she wouldn't have been able to do that for too many nights.

McClain had bought her the rings and paid for the license and the judge who'd married them. He'd also paid for all their meals and the simple but satisfactorily elegant reception brunch, but she'd been determined to take on the few costs left to her as the bride.

Including one last grand splurge to put a handsome wedding band on his left ring finger. She'd managed to get the size right, due to some stealthy observation, and she'd been rewarded by the glimmer of surprise in his dark eyes and the smile that let her know he'd been pleased.

Uncertain of what he'd like, she'd taken a chance on a gold band with an unusual carved pattern. The design had seemed very Southwesterny and Native American to her, and she'd thought the moment she'd seen it that a cowboy might—if he ever decided to wear a ring—choose this one. McClain had worn it every second that day so she relaxed a little, at least over that.

The Cessna smoothly touched down on the airstrip a mile from the headquarters, but her nerves jumped high in painful contrast. She'd been reared to handle herself correctly in any social situation, but she realized suddenly how far out of her element she was. A lifetime of secret insecurity and a need to please others—not to mention her recent financial failure—had undermined her so much that she felt like a dunderhead.

And she hadn't been exposed to anything here yet! Her abiding worry, that the people here were so far out of her experience that she was at a severe disadvantage, surged up. First impressions were vitally important, and she couldn't seem to help that she felt a little more desperate to make a good first impression than she normally might have been.

Particularly when everything she did would reflect on McClain, just as everything he'd done in New York had reflected on her. Thank God, he'd managed to completely charm her close friends, and he'd handled himself beautifully in every situation. Would she be able to do the same?

"You look pale, darlin'. Do little planes make you airsick?"

Stacey glanced his way to see him watching her. The steady search he made of her face let her know he'd catch any nuance. It wasn't in her mind to lie to him, though she didn't want to tell him the whole truth.

"Just a little nervous."

He reached for her hand and gave it a warm squeeze. "Relax. You could step out in a clown suit with a big rubber ball on your nose and folks would like you anyway."

The picture of that startled a giggle out of her

SUSAN FOX   69

and he squeezed her hand again. A small half-smile
played around his sternly carved mouth.

"That sounded a little like music, Miss Stacey.
I hope to hear more."

And then he released her hand to unbuckle his
safety belt and maneuver himself out of the seat
then behind hers to lever open the door. In moments, he was helping her out of the plane as if
she was little more than a small child.

By the time she was on the ground, a pickup
was racing toward them from the headquarters.
The rooster tail of dust behind it boiled up then
drifted across the pasture. McClain was already un-
loading their luggage, leaving Stacey to stand by
uncertainly.

The peach linen suit she'd chosen to travel in
and her peach pumps with delicate heels were
completely unsuitable, not only for the still hot airstrip surface, but also for a ride in a small plane
and a dusty ranch pickup. She might have chosen
something less dressy if she'd known she'd be
traveling in a Cessna and a truck at the end of the
day, but by the time she'd found out, it had been
too late. As a woman who'd always been persnick-
ety about her clothing, Stacey guessed she was
about to face the steep challenge of remaining
clean as well as unwrinkled.

And dry. Though it must be almost seven in the

evening, the air was still as hot as a furnace. She was already perspiring, and after the stress of these past weeks, and the worry and pressure of the past few days, she could feel herself rapidly wilt.

The pickup slowed to bump over the edge of the tarmac onto the airstrip, but the dust cloud moved over with it and billowed ahead to engulf the plane. Stacey could feel grit settle on her from head to toe.

"Looks like we're still short of rain," McClain remarked to the driver, who'd climbed out of the pickup to lend a hand with the luggage.

The two men had their things stowed in the back of the truck in no time. After he'd introduced Stacey to the ranch hand, whose name was Jeb, McClain opened the passenger door of the pickup and took her hand to help her in. As it had been with the Cessna, the skirt of her suit was too tight to step up, but before she could discretely hike it higher to accomplish the deed, McClain caught her around the waist and deposited her neatly on the seat. Stacey scooted to the center just in time for both men to get in on either side of her and close the doors.

"Bert got the homestead rewired," Jeb said as he put the truck into gear.

"Did we get that gelding delivered?"

"He didn't take the trip too well. Put him in a

corral, but he about took it apart. So we put him in a steel pen.''

The blunt Q and A went on all the way to the main house, and Stacey felt both clueless and left out. It surprised her now to realize how much she'd enjoyed the time she and McClain had spent alone that week, but now that he seemed to virtually ignore her, her feelings were a little injured.

Perhaps it was the random nature of the terse conversation about a variety of topics that she knew nothing about. Talk of homesteads, geldings, west pastures, tanks, flywheels, and laminitis raised more questions for her than they answered for McClain, and she felt even more out of her element. Hopefully these things were not as foreign as they sounded, and she'd quickly catch on.

When they reached the single-story main house, Stacey decided she liked the style of it. Its generous size was reassuring, and it had a stateliness and permanence to it that confirmed it had stood for generations of McClains.

Not that she'd doubted McClain's word about the ranch being in his family for four generations, but she hadn't truly expected something on this grand a scale. And because she'd managed to lose the fruits of generations of Amhearsts, it was a small consolation to now be connected to another family heritage of long-standing.

Solid evidence of the fact that Oren McClain's family heritage was proud and evidently durable, and that he'd probably more than done his part to diligently guard and add to it, gave her a sharp sting of guilt. She'd not added a thing to her heritage, and she was the Amhearst who'd been careless enough to let it slip through her fingers. Though the police regarded her as a victim, she'd never be able to accept that she wasn't completely to blame.

Suddenly, marrying McClain made her feel as if she'd escaped the full punishment for what she'd done, as if she'd cheated. And though she'd weathered significant consequences, not a bit of the guilt she'd felt had been soothed.

It was bad enough that she'd married McClain for his money. But she also craved protection and some sort of purpose in life, though when she'd had money, being protected and having a purpose were things she'd rarely thought about.

Modern women saw to their own protection, and they decided their own purposes and goals, then set about forging them. They certainly didn't marry exciting strangers because they needed to depend on someone else for those things.

The condemnations she'd pelted herself with for months rained down with new vigor as she mentally added these new character failings to the list.

By the time the pickup came to a halt at the front of the big house, Stacey's spirits were lower than ever.

The two men immediately got out of the truck and McClain turned back to take her hand as she eased to the edge of the bench seat and prepared to climb down. When he again caught her waist to lift her to the ground, she felt a nettle of irritation.

In New York and all the way here, she'd loved being treated like a fragile piece of porcelain, but she suddenly hated it, and the swing from despondency to anger was a sound shock. Though she'd been too conscious of behaving like a lady to ever allow herself much of a temper, she felt the sharp lash of one now. In truth, it wasn't aimed at McClain so much as it was aimed at herself, but his solicitous care had been the trigger.

Then again, it had been a crazy week, following months of unbelievable emotional trauma. Perhaps now that she was feeling safe, her emotions would be unpredictable for a while. And if she remained true to form, this brief spurt of anger—and resentment—would soon vanish and leave her in her usual tepid mood.

Instead of helping with the luggage, McClain escorted her up the front walk. The arches along the front of the house opened onto a deep verandah with a stone floor. It was accented by flower pots here and there that were crammed with vivid red geraniums that looked hothouse perfect, and the glossy red paint of the double front doors were a match to the flowers.

When they stepped onto the stone and reached the doors, McClain released her to open them and shove them wide. In the next instant, he'd caught her up in his arms.

"Welcome home, Mrs. McClain," he growled, then gave her the kind of hot, demanding kiss that she'd missed getting since the night he'd proposed.

Whatever her seesawing emotions had been, they were scorched away by a flash of carnal feelings and sensations that left her breathless. As if mindful of the ranch hand coming up the walk behind him, McClain abruptly ended the kiss, then carried her over the threshold before she could get her eyes fully opened. After that kiss, she didn't really care where he'd carried her, only that he'd started something explosive then stopped it in a way that left her craving more.

She wasn't able to recover as quickly as he had, and when he lowered her to her feet her knees were amazingly weak. If he hadn't kept hold of her she might have fallen onto the hard tile of the foyer. Self-conscious because the ranch hand had seen it all, including her swooning moment, she made herself push a little away from McClain and turn, so she could pretend to glance around in hope of hiding the heat in her face.

The foyer was like a page out of a decorating magazine, with a proper table and a huge urn that held a cactus taller than she was. A large Victorian mirror was centered above the table and the opposite wall featured an oil painting of a woman in a prairie dress who stood on the porch of a quaint cabin surrounded by fields of sun-baked grass. A McClain ancestor?

Before she could ask, McClain gave her time to freshen up in a hall bathroom, then took her on a tour of the big house that began with an introduction to his cook, Alice, and his housekeeper, Connie. Alice was the wife of the ranch foreman and Connie was married to one of the ranch hands. They both lived in houses on McClain Ranch instead of in the main house, which surprised Stacey.

As McClain showed her through his home she instantly liked the color and energy of it, though it was virtually the opposite of the delicately feminine, pastel and white look of her New York apartment. Dark wood floors featured plenty of thick, brightly colored woven rugs that went well with the heavy masculine furniture.

There were occasional feminine touches—a throw pillow, a vase of silk flowers, ruffles and lace here and there, a painting—but, along with several oil paintings of Western scenes, it was clearly a man's house, furnished with men in mind.

Everything looked substantial and durable, with several pieces that must have dated back generations. Outdoorsmen and ranchers could come and go in a house like this and never feel even remotely like a bull in a china shop. The fact that everything was perfectly clean and well taken care of told Stacey that McClain's household staff took pride in their work.

She was surprisingly pleased with it all, particularly the fact that it was air-conditioned. Once McClain had finished the kiss and set her on her feet in the foyer, she'd registered the welcome chill of the house and any worries she'd had about Texas heat vanished.

The master bedroom was much larger than the other five bedrooms—it was almost a suite—with a breakfast table near the French doors and a short sofa and armchair at the end of the room opposite the foot of the huge bed. All of it radiated a feeling of marital intimacy that she wasn't at all ready for. The two walk-in closets were surprising to find in a house that had obviously been built and furnished with a man's tastes and comfort in mind.

"I see that look," McClain said and her gaze flew to meet the amusement in his. "If you run out of room in your closet, you can always use a little of mine. Just leave me space to hang a few of my things.''

The twinkle in his dark eyes told her how much her vast collection of clothing had shocked him and, no doubt, he was wondering if there'd be any closet space left once all her clothes were unpacked and hung.

''I won't need to have everything in here,'' she said, though she wondered where else she could keep her off-season clothes and extras. Surely there was some sort of storage tucked away in a house this size. Or maybe over the six-car garage that stood well away from the house. On the other hand, she might consider weeding out some of her things.

The thought surprised her because she tended to hang on to her clothing, whether she actually still wore it or not. It was that same bend toward sentimentality that had made it impossible to think about selling her furniture, particularly any that were family heirlooms.

Now that she'd seen Oren McClain's home, she had at least some hope that a few Amhearst antiques might add a nice touch here or there. And perhaps her china and crystal could be used for entertaining, though she had no idea how formal events were at the ranch house. The dining room

had been quite formal, which suggested her orna-
mental crystal pieces might find some use.

It was easier to mentally fit her belongings into
the decorating scheme of McClain's house than to
mentally fit herself into it. A glance in the foyer
mirror had put her reflection next to the one of the
woman in the prairie dress, and Stacey had looked
sharply citified and out of place. She imagined she
looked equally out of place against the backdrop
of the colorfully masculine house.

And that was another reminder of the contrast
between her and McClain. He was big and rugged
and dark; she was small and fragile-looking and
blond. He was all tough, unrelieved masculinity,
and she was soft and completely feminine.

Though that was considered the ideal, it was the
prelude to a long list of less desirable differences.
Their backgrounds couldn't be more opposite, and
their hearts and minds and interests were surely
polar opposites. The sharpness of that contrast
came home to her in a more stunning way than
ever, and she felt the harsh jolt of it.

What had she done? Stacey suddenly felt like a
child who'd asked for strawberry ice cream when
she'd really wanted vanilla. And now that she'd
had a taste of strawberry or seen pulpy little chunks
of fruit in the treat, she suddenly didn't want it.
She'd always been free to reject the strawberry and

revert to vanilla, but she was married now, and her vanilla life was forever gone.

Perhaps the analogy fit in more ways than one. She'd never actually had to be an adult before, at least not an adult with grown-up responsibilities. She'd been an adult of course, but being an adult had never made any real demands on her, since she'd been free to mostly indulge herself in the privileges. Now she'd married a man who was such an adult that it was hard to imagine he'd ever been a child. And not only was he a full adult, he was an adult male.

And there was nothing more adult than the heat in his dark eyes as he leaned back against the open doorway into the closet. With his big fingers wedged into his jeans pockets and the slow sweep of his gaze down the front of her—not to mention the way it lingered on the way back up—he was sexiness personified.

"You've got the look of a lady who's about to panic," he drawled, and she felt a flutter of exactly that.

"I'm thinking...we're so different from each other," she ventured, determined to be as honest with him as she could.

"We were made that way," he said, and his voice went even lower, "and I appreciate that more than you'll ever know."

He'd meant it as a sexy remark and it was, but she hadn't been talking about their sexuality. If her worries had only been about those differences, she'd be far more at ease with all this. She'd been thrilled—completely thrilled—with him as a man so far, however nervous she was about intimacy, but they couldn't spend all their time focused on sex and male/female issues. Just like every other husband and wife on the planet, they'd spend most of their lives together out of bed, and there was almost no common ground between them, other than a marriage certificate.

"I wasn't talking about those differences exactly…" she ventured.

"And I can't think about anything else."

His quick comeback banished everything else for her too, and suddenly her worries about sleeping with him so soon—and consummating their marriage—surged to the surface.

Oh, was there no way to feel comfortable with any subject in her life these days? She felt like a mouse in a maze, crowded between narrow walls, desperate to reach the safety and freedom she'd always known, but doomed by one bad turn after another to a fruitless search for the way that led to escape.

McClain pulled one hand out of his pocket and held it toward her, the look in his eyes persuading

her to put her hand in his. The calloused warmth
had an immediate effect, and a tingling charge
sparkled through her.

"We ought to have supper before it gets too late
so Miss Alice can get home," he said, then added,
"You're too much temptation with a bed this
close."

The blunt words as much as declared that any
hope she'd had about delaying a real wedding
night was futile. Hadn't she known that all along?
A man like McClain wouldn't be the kind to wait
for something he knew belonged to him.

They'd been married today, that marriage would
be consummated tonight. It was just that simple
for a practical, self-confident, overwhelmingly
masculine man like him. And he might have at
least some idea that he was completely entitled.
But whether it was because he thought he'd bought
himself a wife or because he'd married the woman
he'd taken the time and trouble to go back to New
York for, she didn't know. She hoped it was the
latter, but it occurred to her now that she might
never know for sure which it had been.

Another bit of proof that she should have found
some spine and faced the future under her own
power rather than his.

To her surprise, he didn't kiss her, though he did
lift her hand and press a lingering kiss into her

palm. He watched her face every moment, and when he was finished, something shifted in his dark eyes and he drew her along with him to the hall door.

CHAPTER FIVE

THEY had their late supper in the dining room, which had been transformed while they'd toured the house. The long, glossy table had been set with fine china and crystal and fresh-cut flowers. A beautiful candelabra sat next to the flowers, and it cast a warm romantic glow over the large, dimly lit room. There was even a bottle of champagne resting in a bucket of shaped ice.

McClain seated her and set about opening the champagne with an ease and expertise that suggested he'd had more than a little practice. He didn't spill a drop, and quickly poured a conservative amount in two wine flutes.

It was just another indication that Oren McClain was hardly the country bumpkin she'd first taken him for. All week as they'd dined out, she'd come to realize that he was more than adept at knowing which fork to use, and his gallant manners convinced her that he would be completely competent and at ease in any situation. She was a little ashamed to have ever thought otherwise.

And she'd learned that the beautiful tuxedo he'd worn at Buffy's party was not the only one he owned—she'd seen two others in his closet just now—so he'd apparently had extensive practice with formal occasions.

McClain took his place at the head of the table, and she liked that she was seated to his right. She'd shared endless numbers of meals with a grandfather who'd dictated that she sit at the end of their long table opposite him at the head. The custom was part and parcel of the emotional distance she'd been raised with, so she liked the cozier feel of this.

McClain lifted his wine flute and waited until she'd lifted hers.

"Would you like to propose the first toast, or shall I?"

"Why don't you?"

As if he'd preferred to be first, a slow smile softened his stern mouth. "To the next fifty years...and more."

The *and more* wasn't only about the count of years. Stacey read it in the glittering intensity of his dark gaze, and she suddenly felt shy as she touched her wine flute to his and then drank the small amount of champagne.

As McClain poured another shallow measure of champagne, Stacey thought of several possible toasts, but none of them seemed very spectacular, though there was one thing that was certainly a heartfelt hope.

When he was ready, Stacey offered a soft, "May we…be happy all those fifty years to come…and more."

That seemed to satisfy him, and he touched his glass to hers and they drank the toast. Then they started on their supper. It was a fairly common meal of steamed vegetables, baked potatoes and thick, juicy steaks, and perhaps that was because it was the kind of no-nonsense meal McClain seemed to prefer, as she'd seen in New York.

Unlike her vegetarian friends, Stacey enjoyed steak, and though hers had been simply prepared, it was perfectly done. She might not know how to cook, but she certainly appreciated fine cooking.

And perhaps a hefty share of her enjoyment had far more to do with her relief that McClain had a very competent cook and wouldn't need his wife to do it for him. Her worries over that had vanished, just as her worries about keeping his house had vanished the moment she'd seen the size of it.

"I hope you don't mind that we aren't going on a honeymoon right away," McClain said then. The remark surprised Stacey and she glanced over to see him watching her face.

"We've been so busy that I haven't given a thought to honeymoons," she said, and she truly hadn't. Theirs wasn't necessarily a union that followed all the usual traditions, and this week had been unbelievably rushed.

"I've spent enough time away that I need to stay close by for a while," he said. "We'll go somewhere later, maybe after the fall gather."

She had no idea what a "gather" was, so she ignored it for now. "Do you like to travel?"

"The better part of my time's spent here, but I've got someone to travel with now. It's bound to be more enjoyable."

Stacey smiled a little at that. It was a sweet thing to say to a new wife, but it was also a small signal that McClain might be open to a lifestyle change or two if she wanted it.

"Traveling is nice, but I tend to enjoy things closer to home as well," she told him. It was a reciprocal thing to say to him, and she had done it partly to send the message that she was also open to lifestyle changes.

It was also the truth. She had friends who jetted across the world at the drop of a hat, but she wasn't as enamored of that. On the other hand, she'd had a very full social life in New York. Depending on how well she tolerated the isolation of the ranch— and the flight from San Antonio had emphasized that sense of isolation—she might soon welcome more frequent travel.

"In place of going on a trip right away," McClain went on, bringing her attention back to the subject he apparently wanted to pursue, "I'd like us to spend some time together here. I need to stay involved a few hours a day with the ranch, but we can use the rest of the time to get to know each other better."

Stacey couldn't help but be touched by that, but the feeling began to ebb as he went on.

"You need to get used to things, and that includes learning how this place runs. If something happens to me, we both need to know you can take it on. The best place to start is with little things. Like learning to ride."

Stacey stared, taken aback. He couldn't mean that the way he'd said it, could he? Learning to ride was one thing, but the idea that she might ever be expected to run this massive ranch—or need to—was staggering. She'd been worried about having to cook or clean his house, but this was worlds beyond those paltry concerns.

And particularly after her horrible failure to manage her own family's fortune, she didn't want to be responsible for McClain's fortune. This wasn't trust funds and investments, it was ranching and oil and who knew what else? Stacey suddenly felt a little sick.

"You aren't serious..." she began, unable to keep the edge of horror out of her soft voice.

"As serious as a funeral, Miss Stacey, if you'll pardon the bad pun. You're bright enough. Your confidence has a way to go, but you've got it in you to take on anything you want to. And maybe that's the key: anything *you* want to take on."

At first, her brain skipped over the little nettle in the end of that because she'd heard something else that distracted her. Something that made her feel odd and a little flattered, as if Oren McClain had looked inside her and found something admirable that no one else had seen. Something she hadn't seen, but also something she wasn't certain was really there.

Her grandfather had given no sign that he'd ever seen any potential for spunk or competence in her, which might have been why he'd had his businesses liquidated in his last years so all she'd have to contend with was money and trust funds and investments. What McClain had just said indicated he'd seen at least something he considered worthwhile. Either that or he'd imagined it because he'd wanted to.

Didn't he realize she'd married him because she'd failed her responsibilities? She'd told him how she'd lost her money, so she'd taken it for granted that he'd realize she'd married him looking for an easy way out of her mess. After all, neither of them pretended this marriage was about love.

That was part of why she was so staggered by the idea of preparing to take over all this in McClain's place, if need be. Particularly when taking over here would be akin to the notion of stepping in as governor of Texas!

A nervous gulp of water did little to soothe the dryness in her mouth, and eventually she set her glass aside. She couldn't eat another bite of her meal, so she set her napkin beside her plate.

"If you'd like to use the shower first, I can clear the table for Alice," McClain said. It took her a moment to make the mental shift to a new subject and remember that Alice was his cook. Stacey's gaze shot toward the elegant clock on the wall across from her, then back to meet McClain's.

"But it's just nine o'clock," she said, caught off guard again by the suggestion that he expected the evening to end this soon. Since she rarely went to bed before one or two in the morning, she wondered how on earth she'd get to sleep. But then she realized sleep was the last thing McClain had in mind.

"We get up by five out here," he said as he rose to step over and ease her chair back for her, "so it's late at nine."

Stacey stood, flustered. One moment he'd made an announcement that had thrown her into complete chaos, then he'd switched to another subject that was almost as troubling. He clearly expected complete intimacy tonight—perhaps within the hour—but she needed more time to prepare herself emotionally.

Desperate to slow things down between them, she ventured a soft, "Perhaps we could both clear the table? I heard—Connie, wasn't it?—mention some messages in the den." She left it there when she saw the glimmer of humor in his dark eyes.

"It's hard to remember things like messages on a night like tonight."

Stacey's cheeks went hot but she didn't comment. McClain accepted her small delay and took the champagne bucket with him to the kitchen before he brought back a tray.

That was the moment the silence between them became more intense, and the realization slowly began to increase her awareness of the rising tension between them. While McClain took care of putting out the candles, Stacey stacked their tableware on the tray.

It was hard to ignore that the air between them seemed to grow charged. The longer the silence stretched, the more she felt as if electricity were arcing and snapping between them, building volt by volt toward some spectacular peak. Any sensuality between them before seemed almost tame now that this raw feeling of anticipation was in the air.

They went to the big kitchen in that same ocean of charged silence. The sense that the evening was now racing toward those moments not far away when they'd share a bed, was becoming acute.

At least she knew how to load a dishwasher. Too quickly Stacey finished the task and added the soap before McClain closed the door and pressed the buttons to get it started. Then he caught her hand and drew her into his arms.

His gaze was intent as he studied her flushed face. "You're nervous about tonight."

At least he seemed to understand about that, and a faint smile played over his mouth as his voice went lower. "Don't be nervous. I might feel like I've waited years for tonight, but I know it's a little more sudden for you."

She noticed he hadn't let her off the hook. But then, the feeling of being in his arms, pressed against his hard length, was having the same dizzying effect on her as it always had, and she was rapidly melting.

He was her husband now, and he was certainly experienced enough to overcome her natural modesty. Hadn't the fact that he so easily overwhelmed her in the past been part of why she'd shied away from him months ago? But she had the security of marriage now, so being overwhelmed surely wouldn't feel as threatening.

His dark head descended, and his cool, firm lips settled on hers. Instead of the fiery kiss she'd expected, this kiss was coaxing and unrushed. And it didn't last very long, which was a new surprise. Nevertheless, her eyes were slow to open as McClain lifted his head.

"Why don't you go on in and do whatever it is you want to do? I'll be in soon."

Stacey as much as oozed out of his arms as stepped back, and because she worried that she'd somehow freeze up later and not be as strongly affected, she almost wished he'd continued on and had actually started seducing her now. She tried to come up with a smile that didn't look uneasy, though she sensed she'd failed when she saw the faint spark in his gaze.

"I'll try not to be...too long," she said, then immediately regretted that her breathless words had made it sound as if she was hinting that she couldn't wait and that he could hurry in.

She wouldn't be any good at this, no good at all!

As Stacey went to the bedroom end of the large ranch house on legs that felt shaky, she tried to remember everything she'd heard or read about men and sex. Perhaps it wouldn't matter so much if she wasn't good at it.

Oh, who was she kidding? Good sex was a priority with all men, so it had to be an even higher priority with a wildly macho man like McClain.

Glum and half sick, she got her things for bed and shut herself in the large master bath, so troubled over everything that she felt like jumping out of her skin. A quick shower and several minutes blow-drying her hair did little to soothe away her nervousness.

It was too soon. She was terribly fond of McClain, and he seemed to be quite fond of her, but neither of them had so much as hinted that their fondness was anywhere near the realm of love. They had chemistry in spades, and yet they didn't truly know much about each other, not really. Not even as much as newly acquainted friends with common interests.

She'd read articles about how having sex too soon interrupted and stunted the emotional maturing of a relationship, and that early sex had the potential to prevent a relationship from ever deepening. Because she'd always seen sex as the ultimate expression of deep, committed love, she'd hoped this week that they'd somehow fall madly in love.

Though she didn't exactly believe in love at first sight, she did believe deep attraction could rapidly evolve into love. But the fact that it hadn't happened yet for her was a sure indication that it couldn't possibly have happened yet for McClain.

He seemed so intent on advancing the sensual side of their marriage that she was beginning to doubt that love was even a marginal priority for him. He'd as much as declared it when he'd proposed again. What he'd said about chemistry and choice seemed even more significant now.

Perhaps brutally masculine and very physical men tended to assign value only to the carnal side of a relationship and barely gave a thought to the emotional side. Her belief was the exact opposite, but now that bedtime was so close there seemed no chance at all for tonight to be about anything more than sex.

Stacey finished with her hair and briefly checked her appearance in the huge mirror. The satiny white of her floor-length nightgown and matching robe made her look almost untouchably pure. With her blond hair curving neatly to her shoulders, her pale skin, and the vivid blue of her eyes, she was the visual depiction of virginal femininity.

She felt a little relieved by her almost ethereal reflection. Perhaps McClain's eagerness would be undermined by it. She hadn't exactly indicated that she'd had vast experience in the bedroom so perhaps there was still a way to get him to realize how monumental this was for her. And once he realized that, he might consider waiting until stronger feelings developed between them.

Stacey heard a small sound out in the bedroom. It took almost all the courage she had to open the bathroom door and walk out, but she made herself do it before she could lose her nerve. If all else failed, she needed to be mature about this.

But the moment she saw McClain in the black pajama bottoms that seemed to emphasize the width of his broad shoulders and the incredible muscle definition of his hard chest and middle, she felt her courage vanish along with her breath.

His bride was beautiful enough to hurt his eyes, but it was an ache well worth enduring.

After a quick look at his messages that assured there was nothing pressing to deal with, Oren had come to the bedroom to grab a few things and shower in one of the guest bathrooms. To avoid shocking his very nervous bride, he'd found a pair of pajama bottoms to put her at ease.

But then she'd walked out and her pretty blue eyes had landed instantly on the bare expanse of his chest and he saw the slight flutter of lashes that told him he'd shocked her anyway.

But her effect on him more than returned the favor. Dressed in the kind of white satin night-clothes that both concealed and provided tantalizing outlines, all she needed was a set of wings and a magic wand to look like some beautiful fairy princess out of a kid's book. Or an angel.

Oren liked that she wasn't quite the big city sophisticate now. Instead, she looked vulnerable and uncertain and shy. The fine manners that she used to keep herself aloof and safe weren't quite enough to accomplish those things now, and it was plain in the faint worry in her eyes that she knew it.

What she didn't know was that he wasn't quite the oversexed brute she might be afraid he was. It was their wedding night, but he didn't need road signs and a barricade to know she wasn't ready to go as far as he might like. Besides, he had other reasons to make himself wait.

And yet, he wouldn't make any rash promises. As a man who'd prided himself in his sexual self-control, Oren's sudden lack of confidence in that was a surprise. But Stacey was his wife now, and he reckoned it was the whole idea of being married that made him less sure he could hold back. In his mind, marriage was the place to give free rein to sexual desire and he'd looked forward to it.

But not tonight. His good intentions wouldn't last too many more nights, but he not only meant to wait for things to happen more naturally between them, he was waiting for the outcome of something that might be very important to his new wife. And it didn't take instinct to know Stacey would be grateful, both now and later on.

She'd stopped when she'd seen him standing by the bed, and in the seconds that followed, she'd laced her fingers together in front of her. He recognized that as an effort to maintain her calm poise, though to him it looked more like she was trying to hold herself together.

He held out a hand and waited until she'd walked over and put her fingers in his.

CHAPTER SIX

STACEY couldn't take her eyes off McClain's ruggedly stern face, and it was just as well that he'd silently commanded her to cross the room to him and put her hand in his. He'd done that before, and she'd responded automatically, though she wasn't certain if she liked that or not. McClain reached for her other hand then held them both.

"You look beautiful tonight," he rasped in that low drawl that was so sexy and dark. One side of his unsmiling mouth curved up. "Not that you don't look beautiful the live-long day. Just that you're even more beautiful tonight."

And then he leaned down to kiss her softly and Stacey actually shuddered at the bolt of crackling heat that shot through her. Their clasped hands between them kept their bodies apart, but a craving for more of this nonthreatening sweetness made Stacey sway a bit closer.

McClain's mouth eased from hers and she swayed again because she felt dizzy and a little weak. The only coherent thoughts that came together in her brain were, *So far, so good...* and... *maybe this will be all right.*

"Do you want the right side or the left?" he asked, and she opened her eyes to glance up at him, unable for a moment to believe he'd asked that. The question wasn't exactly part of any wedding night seduction she could have imagined.

"I'm...not sure," she said before her brain suddenly cleared and she seized on an idea. "I've never shared a bed."

There. Admitting she'd never shared a bed was as good as hinting she'd never had sex. At least she hoped it was. Though she knew sex didn't necessarily have to happen in a bed, she was hoping that McClain had caught the hint and would perhaps change his plans for tonight.

One corner of his handsome mouth quirked and she saw a spark in his dark eyes that let her know he understood her veiled message. To her surprise, he didn't comment on it, but stayed on the trivial subject he'd started.

"We can always switch sides if you change your mind," he said as he let go of her hands to reach for the belt of her robe.

But once he'd taken hold of it, he did nothing but roll the satin fabric between his thumbs and fingers.

"I like the feel of satin," he said, but then he gave the belt a gentle tug to untie it and let the two ends fall to her sides.

And of course, the facings of the robe went slack and parted. McClain's callused hands eased into the narrow space between the facings and parted them wider as his palms settled on the sides of her waist. Stacey lifted her hands to his hard chest.

Which was a mistake. The hot feel of smooth skin over steely muscle was so amazing that her breath caught. His body was masculinity personified, and everything feminine in her was clamoring with both excitement and fear. He towered over her and the power in his grip alone could have crushed her bones, but the sense of both protection and threat mingled in a way that made her feel so wholly feminine that she felt both weak and powerful.

Weak because her femininity was the delicate counterpoint to his male strength, but powerful because she sensed that she'd somehow captivated him on some very primitive level that gave her control over him.

Stacey felt a heady sense of dominance until he skimmed his hands up her sides then away, and her robe slithered off her shoulders to land in an elegantly rumpled circle around her feet. His palms settled gently on her narrow shoulders before he trailed his fingertips lightly down her bare arms.

The nightgown's bodice was both modest and enticing, with a wide and deep V that ended at the gathered waist. McClain's dark gaze tracked every inch of that deep V before his gaze lifted to make contact with hers again. His rugged face was utterly grim.

"Ladies first," he drawled huskily. The fiery intensity in his dark eyes revealed an almost turbulent desire, and when he stopped touching her, she turned shakily to get into bed, wishing there was someplace more secure to retreat to.

McClain picked up her robe to toss it to a chair, then walked around the foot of the bed to the other side, which gave her time to lie down and pull the comforter and top sheet up to her shoulders.

She caught her breath when the mattress dipped with his weight as he slid beneath the covers, then turned toward her. Instead of rolling closer, he stayed where he was, leaving a mere hand span of space between them, though she felt the warmth of his big body all along her side. He propped his jaw on his fist to watch her flushed face a moment before a slow smile angled across his mouth.

"Your eyes are as big as dinner plates, Mrs. McClain, but supper's over. I can live without dessert tonight."

He found her cold hand with his free one and pulled it from beneath the covers to draw it to his mouth. He kissed her knuckles, then leaned down to place the same kind of gentle fleeting kiss on her lips. He slowly withdrew and she opened her eyes to look up at him.

"There's nothing I'd like better than to do what's usually done on wedding nights, but we've rushed a lot of things. It might be better to slow down a little, catch up on some of the things we skipped."

It was one of the kindest, most thoughtful things McClain could have said, and Stacey couldn't help the deep swell of genuine affection that surged up. Though she'd hoped to be spared intimacy tonight, she hadn't truly expected him to reconsider. And yet he hadn't reconsidered, because she felt certain now that he'd planned this all along.

Her fondness for him took a gargantuan leap toward something far more strong and profound, though she wasn't ready to acknowledge it. Prompted by the feeling, she lifted her hand to place her palm against his lean cheek.

"You're wonderfully considerate, aren't you?" she said quietly. It wasn't really a question, though she'd made it sound like one.

As if he wasn't quite comfortable with the compliment, McClain gave a half-smile and she suddenly sensed he was about to make a joke of it.

"Shucks, ma'am. I reckon modesty prevents me from owning up to all those fine qualities that start with words like 'wonderfully'...but I might take a kiss. Maybe as a sort of reward.''

Stacey hadn't seen this hint of playfulness in him before, and she immediately liked it. She couldn't prevent the smile that burst up from both pleasure and relief. She coaxed him to lean down and when he obliged, she kissed him.

Now that the pressure to have sex had been removed, the kiss became a little more involved. Her arms found their way around his neck, and he moved so close that he was lying half over her. Suddenly the kiss became a near inferno that might have raged completely out of control if McClain had not dragged his lips from hers.

As they both waited for their breath to come back and their racing hearts to slow down, the raw awareness of two bodies pressed together with only a thin layer of satin and a bit of lightweight cotton between, threatened to drive their arousal to a higher pitch.

Again, it was McClain who had the self-control and good sense to pull away and roll to his back. After a moment, he gave a low chuckle.

''That was like two kids playing with matches in a hay barn. They both know better, but they found this tempting book of matches...''

The analogy gave Stacey a peculiar little glow of happiness she didn't completely understand, except that she liked it. She also liked the sweet feeling of deepening affection for McClain.

Her heart chastened her a little for always thinking of him as McClain. His first name was Oren, and though she called him that to his face, she thought of him as McClain. That name was rough, tough and indestructible, and maybe she was drawn to that because she'd needed someone rough and tough and indestructible in her life.

The name Oren was softer, kinder, more vulnerable. It didn't fit McClain at all, and yet it somehow fit him perfectly. Perhaps part of her problem was because she saw *McClain* as someone she needed, but she saw *Oren* as someone she didn't deserve.

That idea had just come together in her thoughts when McClain turned off the light and settled close, distracting her. She felt him take her hand again and pull it toward him. She half hoped he'd kiss her knuckles again, but instead he nestled their clasped hands between them, and Stacey felt another gentle welling up in her heart.

His gruff, ''G'night,'' prompted her to give a soft, ''Good night,'' in return.

It was amazing to lie in the big bed next to McClain—to Oren—holding his hand, marveling at the heat his big body gave off, and at the same time feeling this wonderful sense of comfort and ease.

Perhaps it was trust she felt, and Stacey realized that trust was something she hadn't truly felt for anyone in a long, long time. Now that she thought about it, she wondered if she'd ever truly felt much genuine trust for anyone, even her late grandfather.

But for tonight, she felt it for McClain. It was while she lay there in the dark enjoying the secure feeling being with him gave her, that she drifted off to the most peaceful night's sleep she'd had in months.

Stacey woke up sometime in the night with that same feeling of peace and contentment. That she'd also awakened wrapped snugly in McClain's arms only enhanced those warm feelings. She didn't feel even a whisper of self-consciousness, only a drowsy pleasure that might have lured her back to sleep if McClain hadn't stirred just then. The rusty burr in his voice was soothing, but his words were not.

"Time to rise and shine, darlin'."

She managed to open her eyes a crack, but the room was still dim and quite cool from the air-conditioning, so she pressed closer into the pleasurable heat of his big body, content to stay where she was. After all, it was still night. McClain was either mistaken or he was mumbling in his sleep.

She almost made it back to the depths of slumber when she felt his big hand slide down her back and settle on her bottom. She was only marginally uncomfortable with that until his fingers fanned out and gave her a gentle squeeze.

"Come on, city girl," he rasped. "It's gettin' late."

Jolted a little more awake, Stacey drew back on the pillow to focus on McClain's face in the dimness. His jaw was rough with beard stubble, and his overlong black hair was attractively rumpled, but it was the dancing gleam in his eyes that let her know he was amused.

"You must not be much of an early bird," he concluded. "I expect that'll change in a few days."

Now his palm began to move in a slow circle on her backside and the daring familiarity of that prompted her to move her arm in hopes of gently dislodging his hand. But instead of taking the hint, McClain closed the small distance to her lips and caught them in a bracing kiss.

She was swept away before it ever entered her mind to be cautious, and if he hadn't abruptly ended the kiss and pulled back to turn away and get out of bed, she might have found herself completely seduced.

Wary of how easily he'd slipped past her usual defenses in the early hour, Stacey rolled away to her side of the big mattress and sat up to get her feet on the floor. The alarm clock on the bedside table said it was only four fifty-five and she gave a soft groan.

McClain came around the foot of the bed to take her hand and lift her to her feet. "You can have this bathroom. Wear jeans if you brought any, otherwise wear pants. We'll get you some work gear in town this afternoon."

After that small series of orders, he gave her a nudge in the direction of the master bath before he left her on her own. Still drowsy, she kept moving until she reached the bathroom and shut herself in to prepare for the day.

At some point, she realized she should have taken a few moments to get some clothes, but she waited until she'd done her makeup, brushed her teeth and finished her hair before she came out and went to the closet where her suitcases were.

Last night she'd only unpacked the few things she'd needed, and she realized now that she might not have much time to unpack the rest this morning. McClain seemed eager to start the day so in the interest of goodwill, she needed to find something quickly.

Stacey opened all her cases and left them on the

carpeted floor of the closet to rummage for something to wear. She was glad now that she'd brought
a pair of jeans. She chose a white cotton blouse to
wear with them, and one of her leather belts along
with the pair of black ankle boots she'd brought to
wear with the jeans.

Who knew how long it would take her to unpack
everything she'd shipped to Texas and get it sorted
out? She didn't know where any of it was, and she
needed to remember to ask. It would be wonderful
if Connie took care of those kind of things, but
until she knew what the woman's normal duties
were, it was more polite to assume nothing.

After she found what she wanted and got
dressed, Stacey came out of the big closet in time
to see McClain walking in from the hall. He was
dressed in what must be his everyday ranch
clothes, with a blue plaid Western shirt, wash-soft
jeans and black boots that showed the kind of wear
that told her these weren't the dress boots he'd
worn in New York.

He'd apparently shaved in one of the other bathrooms, and he looked as natural and at home in his
cowboy clothes as he had in his tuxedo and black
suit. His dark gaze alighted on her and swept
quickly to her feet. A quirk curled one corner of
his mouth.

"At least the boots have a good heel, but that

fine leather's gonna get scuffed. We'll find you something else.''

Now he eyed her tight designer jeans and she saw the small war between masculine appreciation and what looked like disapproval.

"And some new jeans and shirts while we're at it." His gaze came up to her hair, which she'd worn loose. "A couple Stetsons and about a case of sunblock and aloe vera."

Stacey had followed all this, mystified, and she glanced down at what she considered perfectly suitable attire. She'd never dressed inappropriately in her life, so the fact that McClain had virtually pronounced her clothes unfit was a shock.

If anyone else had dared to issue such an unflattering commentary on what she'd chosen to wear, she would have been insulted. But she knew nothing about ranch life, so it was best to take McClain's word for it. Besides, the idea that these boots might be damaged wasn't one she liked, since they were her favorites.

The idea of buying cowboy boots didn't thrill her because she doubted she'd like them. Tall boots were uncomfortable in the heat, and these looked heavy, which suggested they'd be clumsy to wear. On the other hand, they looked great on McClain, and he was anything but clumsy in them.

Breakfast was a small feast of steak and eggs,

toast, melon and cinnamon coffee cake, but Stacey picked over her food. She wasn't used to the early hour, which might be why she had no appetite. Though McClain warned she'd be hungry later, she wasn't able to put away even half the amount of food he had. And the coffee was so strong it almost gagged her, so she compensated with water and orange juice.

When they finished, McClain took her to the mudroom next to the kitchen, and the moment she took off her short boots, he saw her opaque trouser socks. He hunkered down in front of her with the first pair of boots.

"Next time, wear white socks. That kind'll burn your feet."

Stacey smiled at how ridiculous that sounded. "What on earth could the color have to do with it?"

"White's cooler, and the kind you need are thick. We'll get plenty this afternoon. And you might want to avoid lace panties. Plain white cotton is best, not synthetic. You'll have to decide about brassieres, but you need something with good support."

Stacey couldn't help her startled giggle. "Pardon me, but I'm wondering how you know all that. Is that common knowledge among cowboys?"

McClain gave a stern look that wasn't completely serious. "You'd be surprised what cowboys know about ladies' underthings, Mrs. McClain. Now let's see if these boots are small enough to fit you."

The pair of boots he'd set on the floor next to her feet looked ancient. After she got them on, McClain did the usual thing that shoe salesmen often did, having her stand, checking to find where her toe was—a task made difficult by the stiff toe box—then squeezing her feet to check the width.

Then he had her walk around to try them out. They were comfortable enough, but they felt odd, and the clomping sound was hardly the kind of crisp, feminine tap she was used to and appreciated. But the underslung heel was a height she liked, and provided a far more stable balance and footing than the spiked or narrow heels she usually chose.

"Those are a good fit, but once you've got the right socks, they'll be a little too snug," McClain said, and when she turned to him, she saw he'd taken a couple of cowboy hats off the far wall pegs. "Let's see about this one."

With that, he plopped the first hat on her head and it dropped down to her eyebrows. He pulled it right off and immediately put on a second. That one fit, and Stacey reached up to test it for herself.

It too felt odd, and she automatically glanced around for a mirror.

"Is there a…" Stacey caught the glittering look in McClain's dark eyes and went silent.

He was obviously waiting for her to say the word *mirror*. It was also obvious that he was amused by the idea that she wanted to see what she looked like in the hat.

"There's one in the hall," he said, so Stacey walked out of the mudroom to find it.

The hat was tan, and she wasn't thrilled with the color. The larger hat had been the right shade of brown to match her boots, but this shade wasn't even remotely appealing. Stacey took it off then bent down to hold it next to the boots to see if the two colors at least harmonized.

McClain's low growl startled her. "Well, I reckon I can finally claim to have witnessed every female peculiarity there is."

Stacey abruptly straightened, and warily glanced his way. For all the disapproval in his low voice, McClain was grinning. "The horses won't care if your hat doesn't match your boots. Let's go."

Embarrassed to be caught doing something that looked idiotic to McClain, Stacey obediently put on the hat—the Stetson—but when she started to follow him toward the back door, she had second thoughts.

"Ah...Oren? I think I'd better make one last..."

She let her voice trail off meaningfully as he glanced over his shoulder at her. A second later, his rugged expression told her he'd taken the hint.

"I'll be on the patio," he said as he walked on, and Stacey didn't need to read his mind to sense that he was again amused with her.

Hoping to be so quick about this that he'd barely have to wait, Stacey started to rush down the hall but then came to a sudden halt. The clomping boots sounded like a stampede of elephants, so she tiptoed the rest of the way to the small bathroom.

On her way back down the hall minutes later, she tried walking as softly as possible, since tiptoeing had pinched her feet. It seemed to take forever to make it out the back door. By the time she stepped onto the patio, she was fairly confident that she was ready for a tour of the headquarters and her first riding lesson.

CHAPTER SEVEN

THE morning air was already warm, but pleasant, and the early sun had added golden highlights to everything. Stacey felt optimistic suddenly, well aware that she hadn't felt genuinely optimistic about anything for a long, long time.

And McClain was so completely gorgeous and sexy this morning—particularly wearing his black Stetson—that when she joined him, she took hold of his hand to prompt him to lean down and kiss her.

He obliged without dislodging their hats, and growled, "Don't tempt me," before he landed a wonderfully hard and brief kiss on her that communicated just the opposite, and elevated her spirits even more. When he drew back, they walked hand in hand toward the far end of the patio.

It was a beautiful morning, McClain was a wonderfully patient and almost indulgent husband, and losing her money suddenly seemed a little less horrifying and tragic than it had before. In fact, the power of the beautiful morning and the exciting presence of the gallant man at her side, gave Stacey the sense that everything would be all right, that she'd never again have to go through anything as hard and embarrassing and frustrating as she'd gone through these past few months.

She finally felt as if her life had taken a major turn for the better, and she was almost lighthearted as the realization began to work its way more fully through her heart and mind. As she walked with McClain toward the ranch buildings, she began to look around with real interest.

Everything was neat and in good repair. She could see cows and horses here and there in the wide network of fences, and the headquarters that had looked huge from the air suddenly seemed even more vast.

At first, Stacey glanced back over her shoulder a time or two to make sure she could still spot the house, because she already had the sense that she might get turned around out here. After all, there were no street signs or traffic arrows, and the scattered assortment of buildings weren't dramatically different from one another in either size or appearance, so they might not serve too well as landmarks yet.

They finally reached the large barn McClain said was the main stable. The wide, hard-packed aisle separated more than a dozen wood-walled stalls on either side. A handful of equine heads loomed out into the aisle from over their stall doors, and all of them swung to look in their direction as she and McClain walked in.

A few whickers that were apparently greetings sounded up and down the aisle, and Stacey smiled a little at the friendliness that suggested. She certainly hoped the animals were friendly, because they were all gigantic.

"You don't need to start today," McClain said, "but it's best you learn to take care of your own horse soon, before you have a chance to develop lazy habits. You'll need to be able to do for yourself out here at some point, because everyone else has their own responsibilities to look after."

Stacey nodded, because it made complete sense that she shouldn't add to anyone's work burden. Surely she could learn to take care of a horse, particularly since they looked fairly self-sufficient to her. She guessed McClain would think more highly of it if she offered to start now.

"Why don't I start today?" she asked, and was rewarded with McClain's look of approval.

"Are you sure?"

Stacey smiled. "Yes. What do I need to do?"

Her question was the prelude to a surprisingly involved tutorial in the proper care of her horse. The one McClain chose for her was a beautiful brown mare with a flaxen mane and tail. After she got acquainted with the mare, McClain talked her through putting a halter and lead rope on the animal. He had Stacey lead the horse out of the stall, then up and down the stable aisle.

Stacey was leery of the mare's huge size, but there was really nothing complicated or difficult about this, so she was glad she'd decided to do it now. Until McClain taught her how to pick up each of the horse's big, iron-shod hooves to inspect and clean them. Then there was a quick grooming that she wasn't so quick with, followed by a hands-on session to put on the saddle.

''Want me to give you a hand with that?'' he asked, and Stacey waved him off. Again, she sensed his approval, which made her surprisingly determined to saddle the mare herself.

A few moments later, she wished she'd not been quite so quick to volunteer. The saddle felt as if it weighed as much as she did, and by the time Stacey got it in place and properly settled, her arms were aching. Tightening the cinches was no easier, and she despaired of ever getting them snug enough. It was irritating that such a simple task could be so hard, but the more irritated she got, the more determined she became to get them tight.

She felt as if she'd accomplished something important when McClain pronounced the cinches tight enough. Then he talked her through exchanging the halter and lead rope for a bridle, and at last she was ready to mount.

While he'd supervised and given instructions, McClain had groomed and saddled his own horse, a muscular red one that he told her was a sorrel. The fact that it seemed to take him only moments to perform the same tasks that had taken her forever to perform, filled Stacey with ambition to do things better next time.

She didn't have time to marvel over that very rare bit of competitive spirit, because her determination suffered a new challenge when she actually tried to mount the big horse.

"I wondered if those britches were too tight," McClain commented when her tight jeans prevented her from getting her foot high enough to reach the stirrup. "I can either give you a leg up, or you can lead her over to a hay bale and mount from there."

Ah, another choice! But Stacey was on to his allegedly sanguine approach and knew which choice he hoped she'd make. Stacey eyed the hay bale and decided she might as well go the whole way and do everything herself.

"I'll try the hay bale," she said, and McClain turned away to mount his own horse with an ease that mocked her inability. He hadn't done it to deliberately mock her, but she felt the nettle anyway.

Vowing to find jeans that wouldn't inhibit her ability to lift her foot to a stirrup, Stacey led the mare to a bale that sat next to a stall wall.

McClain's reminder, ''Mount from the left,'' prompted her to lead the mare into a turn, but getting the correct side of the big horse lined up close enough to the hay bale was frustratingly complex. And even when she'd got the mare where she wanted her, the horse sidled away once she'd stepped up on the bale.

There was nothing but calm in McClain's, ''Take your time. You pulled on the near rein, so she thought you wanted her to do something else. Try again.''

By the time Stacey actually did manage to get in the saddle and made sure both her feet were in the stirrups, her feeling of achievement was thwarted by a glance at the hard-packed dirt floor below. The distance was a little dizzying. Her earlier optimism and determination was rapidly fading, replaced by a few stomach-tightening tendrils of actual fear.

The horse was mammoth. She'd adjusted to the animal's size when she'd been on the ground, but now she was actually sitting on its back, and every small shift of the animal's feet threatened to unseat her. She managed to grip the reins and the saddle horn with both hands, but now the mare was toss-ing her head a little and moving backward.

"Loosen up on the reins, darlin'. She thinks you want her to back up. And she feels your tension, so try to relax."

"I can't do this." The cowardly words slipped candidly out of her mouth, but Stacey didn't care because the mare had sidestepped a little and her leg was about to be crushed between the horse's side and a wall.

Ignoring her hasty confession, McClain calmly repeated himself. "Loosen the reins. She'll stop the moment you do."

Feeling both desperate and angry that she'd fended off so many of McClain's offers of assis-tance that he'd stopped offering, Stacey managed to let a few inches of the leather reins slip free. It must have been enough because the mare did in-deed stop. Now McClain rode his sorrel to her side.

"You can learn to neck rein once we're out-side," he said. "Just loosen those reins a little more and very lightly touch your heels against her sides."

Stacey looked down at her horse's neck as she collected what little courage she had.

"Don't look at the ground," he said. "Look ahead to the open doors."

Patiently, patiently, he talked her through everything. Once she was able to relax and learned the simple signals, Stacey found that the mare responded to everything she did.

She began to enjoy the ride after that—in fact, she loved it—and her earlier optimism came back, along with a rare sense of accomplishment. McClain's lessons were extremely hands-on, and she made a mental note for the future.

Though things had worked out very well this time, perhaps she shouldn't be so quick to take something on before she had some sort of introductory experience. She did like that McClain had watched over her closely, and that he hadn't shown even a speck of impatience or disapproval. That's what she'd liked best, though it had prompted her to try more than she might have otherwise.

By the time they arrived back at the stable an hour or so later, she'd more than caught on and might have liked to keep riding. In fact, they'd ended up riding a full hour because she'd not wanted to stop. McClain had finally insisted, and she got an inkling of why when she tried to dismount.

Her legs refused to cooperate, and she found that even more frustrating than not being able to mount in the first place. Unwilling to ask for McClain's help, Stacey rode the mare next to the same hay bale and kept trying until she managed to get her stiff legs to comply.

But the moment her boot hit the hay bale, her leg buckled and she staggered back against the stall wall. McClain had been standing close enough to catch her arm and slow her descent until she landed on her backside on the hay. Her other boot slipped out of the near stirrup and the mare turned her head to give Stacey a curious look.

"Are you okay?" McClain's glittering gaze told her he was amused, though his mouth stayed a level line.

"All but my pride," she answered. "Will I ever be able to stand up again?"

"Your legs'll recover. Go ahead and try to stand. I'll take care of the mare after I see to my horse."

Stacey managed to stand after a few moments, and as she walked a bit to get her legs working, she watched McClain unsaddle his horse. Figuring she might as well follow through to the end, she started on the mare's cinches, grateful that the unsaddling process went so swiftly. Because she'd noticed McClain give his horse a quick brushing, she did the same.

The effort she'd put into all this was more than rewarded by that feeling of accomplishment. And she knew McClain was pleased with her, which

was satisfying all by itself. Until now, she'd re-
ceived the lion's share of the benefits of this marriage, but if all it took to make him happy was to
take part in this sort of thing, she'd be grateful.

Stacey's optimism about the future began to soar
until they got back to the house and went to the
den.

McClain had neither forgotten nor changed his
mind about teaching her enough about how the
ranch ran so she could one day take over if she
had to. She'd hoped she'd either misunderstood
last night or that the whole idea had been one of
those stray thoughts people often got that came to
nothing.

She should have known McClain didn't indulge
stray thoughts or say something unless he meant
to do it. The rest of their morning was spent in the
den, though his overview of everything was limited
to what kind of files were stored where, the kind
of software he used for this purpose or that, and a
look at his business calendar for the next several
months so she had some idea of the things that
were ahead.

It took almost no time for her to understand that
very little of this made sense to her, and that she
might never be able to grasp even the basics.
Finally she looked over at him, a little dazed, and
he'd smiled as if he'd read her mind.

"Don't fret about it," he said. "Just pay attention and pick up what you can. I want you to know enough to be able to understand what's going on. We've got a foreman, accountants, and different managers. All you need to know is how it all fits together and runs."

Put that way, it didn't sound so bad, and Stacey was enormously relieved. Now that the pressure was off, she was impressed that McClain, macho Texan that he was, wasn't at all the kind of man who meant to keep his woman ignorant and housebound. Or helpless or merely decorative.

And everything today had made it clear that he meant to share his life with her, fully and completely, and apparently without reservation. She couldn't help being touched by that, though it worried her.

She'd enjoyed riding today, and she'd enjoyed being out in the beautiful morning. She'd even enjoyed taking care of her horse, because it was the first time in a very long time that she'd felt at least marginally useful to herself.

But she'd been here less than twenty-four hours. Today these things were an attractive novelty, but what if the attraction faded? She hadn't had time to miss New York yet, or to truly see whether she could tolerate the isolation.

She hadn't met anyone here but the household

help and one ranch hand, so McClain was literally the only person she knew. And now that he was back in his element, McClain was quite different than he had been in New York.

In New York, he'd catered to her and almost coddled her, rarely asking first, just doing things to take care of her. Out here, he made the offer to do something for her, but she'd gotten the sense each time that he hoped she'd refuse and do things for herself.

Could she really adapt to McClain and the life here? She'd essentially pledged to do that when she'd married him, but considering her past habit of growing bored and flitting from one interest to another, did she truly have what it took to stick with this?

If there was anything she'd learned today, it was that every pursuit on McClain Ranch would be encumbered by tasks and chores. And responsibilities, like making certain her saddle was stored where it belonged and her horse properly put away and left with water.

McClain probably thought nothing of these things because he'd done them all his life, and his attention to those kinds of details was automatic and faithfully fulfilled. She'd never even had to make certain her houseplants had water, because someone else had always taken care of that.

Her sobering thoughts lingered during lunch, but their trip into town to buy appropriate clothing distracted her. Though she'd never in her life shopped for work clothes, the small shopping spree soon had the usual effect and brightened her spirits.

Something about spending so much time in the fresh air that morning and again in the late afternoon heat, had worn her out. Normally, being so tired would have spoiled her appetite, but Stacey was famished and had hardly been able to wait for supper to be served. She managed to match McClain bite for bite, and when she'd finally finished eating, drowsiness threatened to put her to sleep at the table.

"Looks like it's been a long day," McClain commented, and Stacey glanced blearily his way. "If you want to get your shower and go on to bed, go ahead."

Stacy doubted she'd ever gone to bed before seven p.m. in her life, but it was becoming harder and harder to keep her eyes open. And her body was stiffening more by the moment, so she wasn't sure she could even work up the energy to make herself stand.

"I don't understand why I'm so tired," she said, "but if you really don't mind, I think I will at least go shower."

The moment she braced her palms on the table to make an attempt to rise, McClain was at her side, helping her to her feet. She barely managed to stifle a groan. Her body had gotten sorer as the day had gone on, but it was so stiff now that the sharp aches were closer to agony.

"You might want to take a hot bath soak out some of that soreness," he said, and Stacey shook her head.

"I'd probably fall asleep and drown. A shower's fine." Now that she was on her feet and the ache of standing up had subsided a little, she moved away from the table.

Who would have thought a relatively short horseback ride could have done this to her? All she'd done was sit while the horse did all the work, but at this point she didn't care if she ever saw another horse, much less rode one again.

McClain took the first couple of steps with her, then let her make her own way to the hall. When she reached their bedroom, she remembered to collect her nightclothes before she closed herself in the master bath to endure the trial of undressing.

She'd gotten her blouse off and unsnapped her jeans by the time common sense kicked in. Her new boots needed to come off first but no matter what she tried, they wouldn't budge. If she tried to pry the heel of one off with the toe of the other, she couldn't lift her knee high enough to add to the leverage. If she sat down on the closed commode to bend her leg to pull them off, her legs cramped viciously.

Hurting and unbelievably irritated, Stacey made herself stand again and reached for her blouse to get dressed. As ridiculous as it was, McClain would have to help get her boots off, and she was too tired and upset to care what he'd think about it.

Every move hurt something somewhere, and that only added to her ire. She'd spied a pair of scissors in one of the bathroom drawers earlier, and she might have been tempted to cut off the awful boots if she'd had enough strength left.

The black, weepy mood was completely unlike her, though self-pity was something she'd become a little more familiar with these past months. Putting her arms back in the sleeves of her blouse reminded her that she was also paying dearly for wrestling a heavy saddle, and that this was part of the price for never going to a gym and working out.

The buttons on her blouse were obstinate, so she only bothered with enough of them to be decently clothed. As she hobbled out of the bathroom to go in search of McClain, pride began to stir.

McClain, Texas cowboy extraordinaire, would surely laugh his head off at her predicament. She knew she'd amused him several times that day, though he'd been too much a gentleman to actually laugh. Yet in all honesty, if these hadn't been her boots that were stuck, she might have at least giggled over it. It wouldn't have occurred to her before this that there was actual lingering pain involved after riding a horse for the first time, and she certainly would have been at least a little amused at someone who couldn't get their boots off.

McClain had probably been riding all his life, so he might not realize how bad she felt. And in the black mood she was in, Stacey didn't want to hear another indulgent comment about city girls or female peculiarities.

Resigned to trying again, Stacey glanced around the big bedroom, looking for something she might use. It was then that she decided McClain might have a bootjack in his closet. She'd seen some at the Western store today, so she hobbled over and opened the door to check. Just as she'd hoped, there was one sitting next to three pairs of boots.

Relieved, Stacey gripped the door frame to help balance herself as she made use of it. But then her foot cramped before she could get it very far up the inside of the boot. She still couldn't lift her leg high enough to clear the top of the boot, so she stood there, desperately trying to press her cramping foot back down into the shoe part of the boot to end this new torture.

Her soft, shamelessly whiny, "McClain!" was probably only loud enough to be heard halfway across the bedroom, but the low voice that answered made her jump at least a mile.

"Those boots givin' you trouble?"

Startled, Stacey jerked to glance over her shoulder, which threw her even more off balance. She might have taken a humiliating tumble to the floor, but McClain rushed forward and caught her arm just in time.

CHAPTER EIGHT

"I SHOULDA thought about the damned boots," McClain said gruffly, and Stacey felt her black, weepy mood vanish. In moments, he'd ushered her to the nearest armchair and sat her down. He stripped each boot off so quickly and easily that Stacey felt only a little discomfort.

"You're gonna have that bath. As hot as you can stand."

Stacey looked up into his stony expression, jarred out of her weary stupor by the sudden inkling that he meant to enforce this edict. Already knowing she'd never be able to get in and out of the bathtub by herself in this condition, she scrambled to dissuade him.

"Oh, no, that's all right. A hot shower will take care of it. I'll be fit in no time."

His dark gaze glittered sharply over her face, and then he grinned. "Liar. You're in agony." Now his grin went flat. "And that's my fault. I shoulda kept that ride short this morning."

Stacey rushed out with, "No, no—it's all right, Oren. I was just having trouble with the boots. After all, they're very new. And stiff." She put everything she had into getting up from the chair without wincing or crying out.

McClain moved back to give her room, and Stacey gave a wry smile to relieve the need to grimace. "I j-just don't want to bend any part of my body. I won't have to bend in the shower." She hesitated, wanting to sound suitably grateful for what he probably considered a kind offer. "But thanks anyway."

She'd made it into the bathroom, though the extra effort involved in trying to move smoothly enough to conceal her pain brought real tears to her eyes. McClain followed her in, easily moving past her to flip the drain lever in the tub before he turned on the hot water faucet full force.

He turned and briefly took hold of her wrist to keep her from sidestepping him, before he started on her buttons.

His low, "This isn't about sex, Miss Stacey, or getting an eyeful," sounded growling and a trifle impatient.

She couldn't help the heat that shot into her face or her wry, "Well, you will be *getting an eyeful,* though I suppose the idea of what an *eyeful* is varies from man to man."

"How about I help you down to your underwear, then stare at the wall for the rest?"

"Ha. I know about peripheral vision, McClain. And mirrors."

He ignored her nervous little jokes. "You can wrap in a towel before I put you in, and you can keep it on while you're in the water. I'll lift you to your feet at the end, then leave while you drop the wet towel in the tub and put on a dry one. How's that?"

Stacey stared into his rugged face as he unbuckled her belt and pulled it out of the loops, but the moment his fingers got to her jeans' snap she felt a bolt of heat in her middle.

"You'd go to that much trouble?" she asked softly, and his fingers hesitated a moment.

"I'm not the one who does laundry around here. If using a bunch of towels will get you in that tub so you can get some relief, then maybe I won't feel like such a thoughtless heel."

That McClain was genuinely upset about this and angry with himself, touched her so deeply that she was suddenly swamped with tenderness for him.

"Oh, Oren, please don't blame yourself. I'm lazy, and I never do anything even remotely strenuous, so this is my fault." Because she didn't feel it was enough to say, she lifted her palm to his lean cheek. "Don't blame yourself. Please."

His hands stilled and he looked into her face.

Just that quickly he leaned close to give her a sweet, soft kiss before he drew back.

"You're unzipped. Do you want a towel before I take the shirt and push the jeans down?"

That he respected her modesty made her feel even more touched, and her eyes stung a little more. "I can wait for the towel."

There was no sense being ridiculous about this. After all, McClain was her husband. And though they hadn't been intimate, having him see her in her underwear wasn't too bad. If she'd worn a bathing suit at a pool, he'd see the same things.

He efficiently dispensed with her blouse and then shoved her jeans down so she wouldn't have to lift her feet more than a couple of inches. He also took care of her socks in the process, and Stacey was affected by the whole notion of being undressed by him.

When he turned away to check the water in the tub and began to adjust the tap to put a little cool water in with the hot, she hurriedly removed her underwear and awkwardly unfolded one of the big towels from the counter to wrap it around herself. She used her toe to push her bra and panties beneath the pile of her other things.

"Have you got that towel on?" he asked, and she told him yes. "Let's get it done."

McClain turned to her and took her hand as she stepped over to the tub.

"Let me try," she said, more leery of being picked up than bending her knees. She braced a hand on him and he gripped her waist to steady her as she got in. Then he leaned close to cradle her securely as he lowered her into the water.

"Too hot?"

"Not bad."

Now that she was sitting, he ran his hands through the water. "You're sure it's not too hot? You don't need to be boiled."

"It's fine. Just no hotter," she told him, but when she tried to ease back against the head of the tub, it was farther back than she'd expected and she grabbed his arm to catch herself.

McClain reached beneath the water level and gripped her waist to move her back a little, then stood and opened a cabinet to take out two other thick towels. In moments, he had one behind her shoulders and the other against the tile to pillow her head.

"Oh, my, this is perfect, Oren. I can't believe how wonderful it feels. Thank you so much."

McClain straightened to tower over the tub. "Looks like those double seams rubbed the insides of your knees. How about farther up?"

"Yes."

"Now you know why you need flat seams on the inside."

She gave a weary smile. "I never would have thought of it."

"And now you won't forget."

Stacey rolled her eyes.

McClain turned away and went to the cabinet. He set a bottle of aspirin and a tube of antibiotic cream, then got out a small round tub of something else.

"After you're out and dry, the cream is for the seam welts. This," he tapped the lid on the little tub, "you can rub everywhere it hurts. But you might as well have the aspirin now."

He opened the bottle and shook out a couple tablets, then filled a glass of water before he came her way with a hand towel to dry her hands before he put the tablets in her palm. He stood by as she got them down, then he took the glass and put it back beside the sink.

Stacey couldn't remember when she'd been taken care of quite like this, except by her nanny when she'd been small. Her memories of her mother were too dim to recall much. One of the maids had usually taken care of things like this when she'd been a teenager, but as an adult, she tended to close herself in her room and hibernate when she was sick or hurt.

McClain was gentle and thorough. He made her feel cared for and her heart opened up to him even more.

"If you have work to do in the den, I'll be fine," she said.

"You almost fell asleep at the table a few minutes ago. And your eyes still look sleepy."

Though she'd planned on soaking clean and showering in the morning, she didn't want McClain to feel as if he had to stay around, twiddling his thumbs until the hot water had an effect.

McClain got her a washcloth and a dish of soap, and set them on the side of the bathtub. "I've got a couple quick calls to make, then I'll be back."

Because he was searching her face as if he wasn't certain he should leave her, she smiled and tried to look a little perkier. "I'll be fine. Go make your calls, but don't feel rushed."

McClain pulled the door partway shut on his way out, and Stacey eyed the soap. She was so, so sleepy, but she made herself lather the washcloth and get started. Promising herself that shower in the morning anyway, she took care of the basics and then managed to work her way over to the faucets to add more hot water to the slowly cooling tub.

She occupied herself with letting some of the old

water out, then adding more blazing hot water, until she was able to move a little more easily. She heard McClain's voice out in the bedroom.

"Are you still awake?"

"I'm fine," she called, but she decided that if he went off again, she'd get out and get ready for bed. After all, she'd turned into a pale prune and she wasn't sure she'd benefit from much more soaking.

"I'll be back in a few minutes, unless you're ready to get out now."

"I'm fine," she repeated, hoping he'd go. He'd done so much already, and she could do the rest herself. And she was a little weary of telling him she was fine, because every time she said it she had a feeling they both knew it was dishonest.

Since she heard nothing more, she carefully got up. McClain had tossed down a terry bath mat, so she stepped out gingerly on it, pleased that everything worked much more smoothly with far less pain. She dried off and applied the antibiotic where she needed to, then slathered the liniment everywhere she'd hurt, even her arms.

The welcome heat was even more soothing, and the concoction didn't smell much at all. She dressed in her nightgown and then turned back to flip open the drain to let the water out of the tub. The least she could do was try to wring some of the water out of the towel she'd worn in the tub, so Stacey made the monumentally difficult effort of trying to squeeze the thick, heavy fabric. Unable to do very well with it, she left it in a heap in the tub and put the other towels and washcloth in the hamper.

The moment she'd brushed her teeth and stepped out into the bedroom, she saw the down-turned bed. She thought about sitting in one of the armchairs to wait for McClain, but she was practically weaving on her feet.

If she could just lie down, she might be able to stay awake long enough for McClain to come back. Keeping the lamp on should help. It felt so good to lie down and cover up to ward off the chill from the air-conditioning that she gave a relieved sigh. And promptly fell asleep.

Oren came into the bedroom and saw that his wife was already in bed and sound asleep. Her cheeks and nose were a little sunburned, as were the backs of her hands, despite the sunblock and aloe vera she'd put on that morning and afternoon. She looked angelic, but she also looked young and innocent. And frail.

Too frail for a brute like him.

He'd seen so much of her being here as a project to improve her, to bring out the character and spirit he'd seen in her. He'd disapproved of the way she'd lived her life—and hadn't really lived— while assigning purpose and superior worth to his. As if her life had been useless and his valuable. He'd set out to fix that because he'd fallen for her.

But Stacey wasn't a failed ranch operation or a misused or abused horse that needed proper management or retraining to make it count for something. She was a woman with flaws and failings and fears that she needed to find her own way through.

She was also a woman with beauty and grace, who was kind and gentle and sweet. She hadn't needed some know-it-all to barge into her life and drag her through some character-building program to fix or improve her.

And that was why he felt like an arrogant jerk. In essence, he'd married a woman to make her over into his idea of what she should be like. Because she'd been unhappy, even when she'd had money, he'd thought she might find something fulfilling with him. A purpose and a challenge that were more important than having the most stylish clothes or indulging every whim or going to fine parties. A purpose more worthy of the woman who'd managed to capture his heart.

But after little more than a day of being married to him, she was exhausted and hurt, so crippled up from riding that she could barely function tonight. He'd been too hard on her, he'd expected too much. He'd known she wanted to please him because she felt indebted, so he'd given her a choice about what she wanted to do, knowing which she'd feel obligated to choose.

His manipulations had brought her to this. Stacey wasn't strong enough or nearly fit enough. He'd known that but he hadn't taken it seriously. That's why she was dead asleep before sundown.

And that was also why he meant to give up his expectations—all of them—and back off.

When Stacey woke up that next morning, a glance at the digital readout of the alarm clock on the bedside table told her she'd overslept. It was five-fifteen!

And she was alone in the big bed. McClain's pillow was dented and his place was still slightly warm, so he'd been here. Disrupted by the fact that he'd already gone, Stacey got up stiffly and walked to the big bathroom. After what he'd said about early mornings, she was surprised he hadn't awakened her.

Feeling rested and worlds better than she had last night, Stacey raced to get ready for the day, choosing the new jeans Connie had laundered and one of her new chambray shirts. It was a little difficult to get her new boots on, but movement was already loosening up her stiff muscles.

She rushed out, hoping McClain was still at breakfast, and got to the dining room just in time for Alice to serve the food. McClain was refolding his newspaper to set it aside when Stacey crossed to her chair.

McClain rose to seat her, and his voice was gruff in the early hour. "You didn't have to get up so early."

Stacey knew immediately what was going on and felt a pang. "You haven't given up on me already, have you?" she asked mildly as she reached for her napkin.

It took him too long to answer, which confirmed her guess.

"I let you overdo yesterday," he said, then corrected himself. "No, I pushed you to overdo."

Overdo. A parade of other times—rare and long-ago times—when she'd overdone things, went through her mind. The time she'd gone roller skating and skinned her knees, the time she'd fainted during a volleyball tournament at school because she'd had the flu and tried to play anyway. The time she'd sprained her ankle learning to ski. Small things that hadn't fazed other parents, but which had sent her grandfather into orbit and resulted in her being banned from further participation.

"You certainly didn't push me to do anything," Stacey said as she spread the napkin on her lap. "And I enjoyed riding."

"It was too much for you. Too soon."

Stacey reached for her orange juice, then hesitated as she remembered other conversations.

My dear Stacey, you're so fragile, so willing, but this isn't for you... Leave that to someone who has an aptitude for it... People who can do that are a dime a dozen.

Any true spirit of curiosity or adventure had been impossible to maintain in the face of an autocratic grandfather who wasn't above resorting to cruel, cutting words if she persisted in something not to his liking.

Could McClain be like her grandfather after all? She'd thought he was the last man on earth to be like that, but perhaps yesterday hadn't been quite the successful beginning she'd thought it was.

It was the word "overdo" that she couldn't stop thinking about. *You know what happens when you're foolish enough to overdo...*

And how could she forget the consequences?

Since I can't trust you to be sensible... You're no good at that... Why would you want to shame yourself again?... You looked like a ninny... Ridiculous...

Stacey decided to do some pushing of her own. "I was hoping to have another try today."

McClain's gruff, "Not today," gave her worries more substance. She took a sip of juice and set the glass aside.

"I thought you said I'd do even better tomorrow. That's today."

She made herself watch him. His dark eyes met hers once then fell tellingly to the serving dish he passed her. "You need to stay at the house today, maybe a couple days. Heal up some before you ride again."

Stacey took the meat plate and helped herself to bacon and sausage. "Nonsense," she dared, injecting just the right amount of lightness and unconcern into her voice. "I'm much better this morning. The more I move, the easier it gets. I look forward to riding. And maybe improving."

Now McClain braced a forearm on the table to give her a stern look. "I saw you last night. You could hardly move without tearing up."

Stacey felt something inside her wilt a little. It was one thing for him to be concerned and want to spare her discomfort, but she was afraid it was more than that.

"It's not because you can already tell that I'll never be any good at riding, is it?"

"You were on the horse less than an hour."

"And that's my point. I wasn't riding all day. Last night didn't prove that I can't learn to ride well, it just proves that I'm not very athletic. I don't jog or work out, so of course I'd be a little sore," she said then paused when she saw his expression harden. "If I ride again today, I'll not only get stronger, but I'll also get some practice grooming and putting the saddle on, which I also need to do better and faster."

"I won't see you crippled up like that again," he said, and there was a dismaying hint of harshness in his tone. "No riding today, and maybe none tomorrow. After that, we'll keep it to twenty minutes or so for a few days. As you adjust, you can ride longer."

Stacey couldn't help feeling frustrated. She'd be willing to bet that no one in all of Texas was coddled like that. An alien feeling of rebellion made it impossible to subside.

"I'm stronger than I look, Oren, and I'm capable of deciding what I can handle and what I can't," she said, careful to keep her voice calm.

She wasn't truly certain about decisions like that because she routinely assumed she could handle very little in the way of challenges, particularly physical ones. Though she had no real confidence that doing something different now would turn out much better, her old way of facing life had made a mess of things.

McClain leveled his stern gaze on her again, and she could tell he might be more than a little irritated. "You think so?"

The challenge was there, the hint of warning was there. Suddenly Stacey didn't know why she'd gone on. Lord knew she was a coward and almost never faced anything difficult or demanding if she could help it. And yet here she was, on the verge of arguing to be allowed to do something that had already proven to be too much for her body.

McClain was probably right. It might be wiser to wait a few days and take it slower. Did she want to put herself through more agony? McClain was the expert with horses and riding, she certainly wasn't. He seemed to think she was asking for trouble, but which choice would cause her the most trouble? Going on as she always had or putting herself to the test?

McClain's gruff question, *You think so?* still hung between them.

Her soft, "Yes," sounded more certain than she felt, but she sensed as she said it that this was vitally important. After a lifetime of being frivolous and self-indulgent and automatically shunning anything that wasn't completely to her liking, Stacey felt compelled to make this change and

stick with it. After all, learning to ride a horse—
and surviving the effort—wasn't exactly brain sur-
gery or saving the world.

She offered a small smile she hoped would ease
some of the tension between them. "I'm a
rancher's wife now. You wanted me to take part
in things here, to learn how it all works."

She kept her smile in place as she went on. "So
far, I've got a bit of a sunburn, a couple welts and
some sore muscles. Taken together, they all
amount to exactly nothing, except that I inconven-
ienced you last night. But other than that, so
what?"

Hearing herself say it that way seemed to give
her courage and put everything into perspective, at
least for her.

McClain's expression had gone so grim that
Stacey was driven to go on, aware that she felt
more passion about this than she'd felt about anything for a long time.

"But the real 'so what' is that I managed to do
everything you told me to, I managed to stay on,
and I actually *enjoyed* it, Oren. I enjoyed riding
that horse. Every minute and every second. I enjoyed it, and I felt good. I've been worried I
couldn't fit in here, that I wouldn't like anything.
But I liked that, Oren. I liked being out in the beau-

tiful morning. I liked it all so much that I want to do it again today. All of it.''

Suddenly aware that her voice had risen with the force of her conviction about this, Stacey abruptly went silent. Oh my! She was making quite a tempest over something that would be minor to everyone else. And certainly would to McClain. Riding a horse for an hour was barely enough to even take note of in his world, where cowboys stayed in the saddle all day and never thought a thing of it.

Stacey looked away and impulsively reached for the bowl of sliced melon to help herself. McClain was still silent, but she could feel the pressure of his gaze on her. He probably wondered what kind of loony she was, and/or he was having major second thoughts about marrying her.

"All right, we'll ride today."

The low words sent her gaze winging to his. Stacey searched his solemn expression, looking for disapproval but finding it frustratingly neutral. Until a faint smile eased over his mouth.

"I reckon you'll do, Stacey McClain."

It had to be some cowboy version of ''You're okay,'' and Stacey smiled cautiously, relieved. And then the first small sparks of excitement began, and she felt as if something new and very good was beginning.

CHAPTER NINE

THOSE next few days were indeed very good, and settled into a varying pattern that Stacey thoroughly enjoyed. Mornings started with a ride after breakfast, then a trip to one place or another on the ranch via a pickup. She even got to drive a tractor, which was ridiculously fun. Particularly because the tractor had a big blade on the back, and she'd gotten to grade a few shallow ruts out of a ranch lane.

Afternoons were spent in the den with business, and every day there were different things to deal with. Evenings weren't only spent at home. Sometimes they went to town to have supper at a local restaurant. One evening, they went to a barbecue on one of the nearby ranches, and Stacey got to meet several of McClain's neighbors.

She'd noticed that McClain's friends referred to him as Mac or Orie. She saw for herself that he was respected and very well liked, and it touched her that the affection people had for him was automatically conferred on her without reservation.

Almost overnight, invitations came for one thing or another, and McClain let her know he was looking forward to her arranging similar get-togethers on McClain Ranch.

Two mornings they didn't ride because McClain flew them to Ft. Worth for a cattle sale. They'd stayed over to see a rodeo, and of course McClain had taken her shopping at Neiman Marcus in nearby Dallas.

A bit of time here and there was spent unpacking her things from New York, which had been stored in the big garage, and each time an Amhearst painting or antique found a place among the furnishings in Oren's big house. Connie helped unpack and hang her summer clothes in her closet, while her winter things were divided up between two of the guest-room closets.

Bedtimes always featured a long soak in a hot bathtub as her body continued to react to the ever-increasing demands she put on it. After a couple of weeks, the lingering soreness dwindled until the long, hot baths were more pleasant habit than necessity.

No two days were exactly the same, and Stacey was surprised to realize how little she missed her old life in New York. Though it seemed she was busy doing something every minute of the day, it was the most peaceful and contented time she could ever remember, and the deepening relationship between her and McClain grew sweeter by the moment.

But there were two flaws in it all that soon began to nettle her. The second most worrying flaw was that the consummation she'd expected since their wedding night nearly a month ago hadn't happened. The sexual tension between them was often so explosive that it came close to going over the line, but McClain always drew away at the last moment, or rarely, tempered his kisses before they could lead to more.

If things hadn't been going so splendidly between them otherwise, Stacey's worry about that might have been much deeper than it was, although it was still a concern.

But the biggest worry, and the one that was truly deep, was that no matter how companionable they'd become, she had yet to hear him declare anything along the lines of "I love you."

Of course she hadn't said anything either, but she was crazy about him now, and it was all she could do to be patient and wait for the right time to tell him so.

In the end, seducing McClain was a sudden decision. It made complete sense to her that he would declare his feelings at some point during intimacy, just as she would. It encouraged her that he seemed to be having more and more trouble stopping things between them, and that the tension she felt in him had also led him to break off his kisses far sooner and more abruptly each time.

Though she was still a novice at anything much beyond kissing and she'd never fit the image of a seductress, she felt strongly that it was time to try something new. She'd tried so many other new things this past month and she'd had enough success at those to think she might be successful with this too.

Stacey stood in front of the mirror in her closet, fretting as she held up the nightie in front of her and debated. She'd bought the scandalous little pale pink pajamas when they'd been in San Antonio the other day. It had been a just-in-case situation, which meant she'd seen them then bought them "just in case" she had to resort to them.

The spaghetti straps looked impossibly frail, but they held up such a bit of nothing that they were more than sufficient. The bodice dipped low and the hem of the top only went down to just below where the waist of the matching panties would be. The diaphanous fabric barely concealed anything it covered, so it was her best choice for tonight.

If McClain didn't get the hint with this, the next step would be nudity, though the pajama's sheerness reminded her that the difference between wearing it and wearing nothing amounted to little more than semantics.

But what if he simply kissed her good-night and rolled away to go to sleep as he had the past handful of nights? Stacey wasn't certain her ego would survive it if she made too big an effort and he still turned away.

Nervous about that, she lowered the nightie and stared at the plain chambray shirt and jeans she had on. She looked country and quite wholesome in the clothes she'd worn since her shower just before supper.

She looked down at the froth in her hands and finally decided it wasn't her style at all, though it was an indication of how worried she was about the whole issue.

Because the thick carpet had muffled McClain's bootsteps, she hadn't heard him come into the bedroom. When he spoke, she jerked in guilty surprise.

"What've you got there?"

Stacey glanced his way, her face going hot as she turned toward him and slipped the pajama set behind her back.

"Oh, ah...just a...nothing important," she said, then walked toward the open closet door, managing to veer a little out of his line of sight to toss the wad of fabric toward the corner on her way out.

"You dropped something," McClain said, then stepped past her into the closet to walk to her cheval mirror halfway down the aisle.

Stacey turned and saw that she'd dropped the pajama's sheer panty in front of the mirror. She briefly clapped a hand over her mouth in dismay as he bent to retrieve it. When he turned and held it up to look at it, she was mortified.

But mortification was too mild a word when he chuckled, and started toward her. His gaze dropped to the floor on his way out of the closet and landed unerringly on the discarded top in the corner inside the door.

"And what's this?"

Stacey couldn't miss the exaggerated curiosity in his low voice as he leaned down to pick up the top. She squirmed inwardly when he straightened and took a moment to sort out the straps, hooking one on each index finger to hold the nightie up for inspection.

"This is so thin I can see you through it, darlin'."

Stacey couldn't quite stifle a gurgle of hysteria and embarrassment. He lowered it a little and looked at her over the bodice. His expression had gone solemn, but humor lingered in his dark eyes.

"Did I spoil a surprise?"

She managed to get out a sound that was more an incoherent squeak.

"N-not really," she said as she stepped forward to snatch it away from him. Embarrassed, and now a little angry, her frustration with both of them slipped out.

"I decided if I had to wear something like this to seduce you, then maybe I don't care if we nev—"

Stacey cut herself off, horrified that she'd put it that way. More rattled than before, she tried to backtrack.

"*Of course* I *care* that we haven't made love. It's just...if it takes something this tawdry to seduce you the first time, then maybe I don't *want* to make love under those circumstances."

A swift mental review of what she'd just said so shocked her that she wadded the bit of nothing and impatiently threw it to the floor.

"That's *not* what I mean either—oh, I don't know *what* I mean! Except that I wonder why a month's gone by and we've never..." She gave an impotent wave of her hand, but then the worry she'd tried to suppress came boiling out in a candid torrent.

"I'm beginning to wonder *what* you feel—what either of us feels. Do I need to pass muster with something? Because I'd like to know where I stand—I *need* to know where I stand. Do we have a marriage, or just a very long, *frustratingly* long, date?''

The stillness that came over McClain worked on her like a dash of cold water. His rugged face had gone stony and the amusement she'd seen in his eyes no more than seconds ago had vanished. His gaze was smoldering now, and he suddenly looked a little dangerous, almost fierce.

She read it in his eyes when his civilized veneer fell away and he became primitive male...primitive and one-hundred-proof sexy.

Stacey held up a wary hand and let out a horrified giggle. ''Oh, I'm sorry. I didn't mean to put it that way. I'm just...upset. Un*reason*ably upset, and I have no idea why.''

''Bet I can guess.'' McClain's quiet words were more growl than speech and gave Stacey such a jolt that she almost strangled on her next breath.

''Oh, no, I...I misspoke. Bad choice of words, *really* bad, and I think I gave you the wrong impression.'' The nervousness she felt showed in an uneasy smile as she took an edgy step backward. ''No—I *know* I gave you the wrong impression.''

''Sounded like the truth to me.''

His low voice still had that growling quality, but she got an inkling that he wasn't angry so much as he was...teasing her? McClain took a small step forward, and Stacey felt a corresponding jump in her heart rate. Fear? Thrill?

"Well…yes and no," she said, and another nervous little titter tried to get free, "but mostly no. Either way, it isn't a challenge to your…to you."

Now McClain smiled faintly, but it wasn't entirely because of amusement—or was it?—and she took another edgy step back. Rising excitement and uncertainty were mingled so strongly that instinct was screaming at her to flee, to run.

Which was ridiculous. She wasn't in any real danger from McClain, but she'd never seen him like this, so she couldn't be completely certain. She wasn't sure how to handle him, so she opted for that familiar standby, cowardice. Stacey turned as calmly as she could to start for the safety of the more public parts of the house.

Except that at this time of night, Connie and Alice were long gone.

"You goin' somewhere?"

Stacey glanced over her shoulder and slowed, though she kept moving toward the hall door. "J-just out—to the living room. There was a news program I wanted to see."

"I've got all the news you need, Miss Stacey." Now the growl in his low voice had gone raspy, followed by a slow, sexy smile that was so wolfish that she knew better than to trust it.

And she couldn't think of a reply, at least nothing remotely coherent, and with nerves and mortification and this wildly thrilling combination of anticipation and feminine anxiety, it was impossible to keep back a rush of nervous giggles.

"I'll never ask 'What news,' McClain," she dared, almost defeated by more giggles, but she couldn't seem to help that she was moving more quickly toward the door. "I'm going to watch TV."

In less than three strides, McClain caught her up in his arms and turned toward the big bed. He paused to playfully give her a series of growling pretend bites on her neck, that made her laugh uncontrollably.

And then he put her in the middle of the bed and followed her down, nibbling at her neck then unbuttoning her blouse to kiss a little more until her giggles wound down to gasps of delight and his lips came back up to take possession of hers. The playfulness between them rapidly changed to something far more serious.

McClain lifted his head and looked down into her pleasure-dazed eyes for several heartbeats of time before he studied her flushed face. His dark gaze slid lower to survey what he'd already uncovered before he brought his hand up to slowly uncover more.

After that, his kisses grew more intense and deep before he trailed them down her throat to explore and tenderly place an invisible mark to claim whatever he wanted. It seemed to take no time at all before she was moving beneath him, clutching him, slowly going wild beneath the power of his lips and hands.

The warm cocoon of complete intimacy wrapped tighter and tighter around them, exposing a bit of this soul to a bit of that soul, touch by touch, soft breath by soft exhalation until slowly, gradually there was nothing between them.

And just when she thought there could be no more wonder, their flesh joined in the age-old way that men and women had joined since the beginning of time, and their souls soared toward the heavens. The dizzying wonders in that high, high place consisted of at least a million glittering lightning bolts of pleasure and delight. The wonders reached a breathless intensity almost beyond enduring, then lingered with a sweet, sweet fervor for a scattering of seconds before each one slowly twinkled away like fading fireworks in a night sky.

The roaring hush in the silent room was the fitting place for racing hearts to slow, and for the languorous sweetness to continue to ebb quietly away until later, when need arose and they again went in search of that high place.

*   *   *

Those next days were the most wonderful of Stacey's life. There was a special quality of closeness that had come with full intimacy, an ease between them that Stacey could never have anticipated, and their daily habits changed to accommodate the differences.

They were rarely out of each other's sight, and they did all sorts of new things together, including showering and skinny-dipping at the creek. They found romantic little getaways on the ranch, and fell into the habit of lying in the back of a pickup truck in one of the pastures after dark to look at the stars—when they weren't doing more delightful things.

The only thing that prevented it all from being a complete heaven on earth was that neither of them, no matter the intensity of their passion, had ever exchanged that singular confession spoken by every other pair of lovers on the planet.

Stacey had consoled herself with the thought that McClain must love her because she was certain she could see it in his eyes, and all the things he did were the acts of a man in love.

Everything was so perfect between them that it *had* to be love. And she loved McClain almost unbearably, though she couldn't quite bring herself to say it in so many words, however many opportunities there were to do so.

It was the final risk in a relationship that had started for all the wrong reasons, yet had turned out to be monumentally lucky and so wonderfully blessed that Stacey was a little afraid that actually saying the words, ''I love you,'' might jinx it.

And then suddenly the day came when those unclaimed opportunities came to an unexpected end.

The phone call had seemed to come out of the blue, though Stacey soon found out that it had only been out of the blue for her. They were just coming into the house an hour before lunch when Alice took a call on the kitchen extension.

''It's for you, Miss Stacey. Long distance. Do you want to take it in the den?''

''Sure. I'll go right in.'' Stacey hung her hat on a wall peg then made a quick trip to the hall bathroom on her way to quickly wash her hands before she went on to the den.

Wondering which of her friends from New York could be calling, she picked up the receiver and drawled a carefree, ''Howdy there,'' that would be sure to get a smart remark.

But the caller was male, and he was all business. ''Mrs. McClain? It's Detective Warren, N.Y.P.D., and I have some news about your case.''

It took Stacey a moment to make the mental

switch from what she'd expected to this. News? She reached back for the big swivel chair behind the desk and sat down.

It was just as well she was sitting, because the news was not only good news, it was incredibly good news. Stunned, Stacey listened closely, so intent on every word that she barely noticed McClain come in and sit down in one of the wing chairs on the other side of the big desk.

Even then, it wasn't until the detective mentioned ''Mr. McClain'' that her shocked gaze found his and fixed there. The call ended fairly soon then, and after she mumbled a dazed, ''I'll be there as soon as I can,'' Stacey hung up the phone.

It was as if the shock had knocked all the strength from her body. If she'd been standing, her legs would have given out. As it was, Stacey sagged back in the big chair as she replayed the conversation in her mind. She might have pinched herself if she hadn't suddenly wanted to hear McClain's admission.

''You hired an investigator to go after my embezzler?''

McClain looked somber. ''You're my wife. I had the means to see if someone could find him. Because of procedure, law enforcement can't always track as efficiently as someone private, particularly in a foreign country.''

"Detective Warren said that your investigator found him, then worked with N.Y.P.D. and authorities in Brazil to arrange extradition. And they got my money back. Not all of it, but more than enough.''

"How much is more than enough?''

Stacey grinned then, so relieved and thrilled that she couldn't help saying, "Enough that, with reasonable management, there'd be very little difference between the lifestyle I led before and the one I could...''

Her voice trailed off. The grimness about McClain told her he'd got the message loud and clear, but perhaps not the one she'd meant to send. Alarmed, she got up and rushed around the desk to go to her knees in front of him and take his hand.

"All that means is, I didn't lose the Amhearst fortune. And the last Amhearst is no longer a pauper. I'm still your wife, only now I'm your rich wife.''

"Everything I own is yours, Stacey, and it was from the day we married,'' he said solemnly. "You were rich yesterday, a multimillionaire. Today you're even richer. What today really means is that if you have any doubts or second thoughts, you wouldn't have to wait for a divorce settlement to go back to living the way you always did.''

Stacey stared at his stony expression, not sure what she'd done or said that would make him automatically put it like that. She was thrilled and relieved and almost joyful over this wonderful news, but now she was afraid to let much of it show because she couldn't have found joy or relief of any kind in his dark eyes if she'd had a week to look. In fact, there was a certain flatness there and a hint of resignation that gave her a sick feeling.

She was trying to find a way to ask him about it when he squeezed her hand and smiled. ''When do you think you could get some things together to leave for New York?''

His smile confused her, because it banished the flatness and there was at least a faint spark of excitement. Or was it simply interest? She smiled cautiously back.

''As soon as I can shower and throw some things in a bag. How soon can you be ready?''

The sick feeling surged when he shook his head. ''I've got that sale to go to tomorrow. That'll mean two days in Ft. Worth, then there's the board meeting at McClain Oil that I can't miss.''

''Then I can wait.''

Now his smile quirked and he shook his head.

"You'll drive me up the wall waiting. I can fly to New York in about four days if you're still there."

"I don't want to go without you."

"And I can't get away, baby. I'm sorry." Now he leaned forward to take both her hands. "You need to go see about this, get everything taken care of. Make your attorney earn his fee. Better yet, get a new attorney. Our attorney here can put you in touch with the right one in New York. I'll give him a call and get you a list while you pack."

Stacey reached up to take his face in her hands. "Oh, Oren, there aren't enough words to express how grateful I am to you for all this. If you hadn't hired someone, who knows if this would have happened? And even if the authorities had found him, it might have taken so long that my money would be gone."

McClain smiled a little, and though it wasn't obvious, she caught the hint of...sadness? "The only thanks I want is for you to come home to me when the dust settles."

"Where else could I possibly want to go?" she asked then kissed him, suddenly feeling a little frantic to assure him that this changed nothing between them and that there was nothing she wanted more than to come home to him and McClain Ranch.

After that kiss, McClain sent her off to pack

while he called the airlines. Stacey assumed he couldn't get her a flight until much later in the day, but after she'd showered and packed enough to last a few days, they had a quick lunch before he drove them to the airstrip.

They flew to San Antonio and had just enough time to land and check in her luggage before she had to kiss him goodbye and start through security. The big airplane had lifted off and reached flying altitude before the sickness came back.

And she deserved to be sick, because Stacey realized then that the very last thing she should have done was hare off to New York without McClain.

CHAPTER TEN

No GOOD deed goes unpunished.

On the surface, the old saying seemed appropriate for the situation, but Oren rejected the notion.

His deed hadn't been that good; there'd been too much self-interest in it. Yes, he'd hired one of the best international investigators he could find, but it had taken enough time for the promising leads he'd initially uncovered to pan out that, thanks to his desirable wife, Oren hadn't been able to hold back on his other private agenda.

It was because those first leads had looked so promising that he'd initially waited to make love to Stacey. If she could get her money back, he'd thought it only right to wait so she'd have a clear choice about what she wanted to do with it. And with her husband.

Because his original thought about making her over had been so out of line, he'd meant to be more scrupulous about the rest. But time had gone on. And on. Until that night he'd caught Stacey plotting to seduce him.

He should have told her about the investigator from the beginning, but he hadn't wanted to get

her hopes up. Losing her money had already dev-
astated her. And there'd always been a chance of
nabbing the thief and not getting back a dime, so
there was no sense putting her through the extra
suspense. She'd been facing enough of that with
the police working the case. If she'd known about
the PI, she might have hoped too much.

Instead, she'd accepted the idea of making a new
life with him. Would she have invested in things
here if she'd thought there was an extra chance of
getting her old life back?

It might only be because she'd had nothing to
go back to that she'd taken an interest in the ranch,
but she'd adapted to everything so quickly and en-
thusiastically that he'd selfishly not wanted to jeop-
ardize it.

Though he'd finally weakened enough to make
love to her, he'd been reluctant to confess his feelings. If she got her money back and decided to
leave him, at least he'd have some pride left. And
since he was certain she wouldn't keep a love confession from him, her silence on that score was
telling.

She'd said plenty of affectionate little things using the words "like" or "fond." And then there
was his favorite: *You know? I could be crazy about
a man like you.* Stacey had plenty of cute ways of

saying things, but nothing close to a love declaration. So he'd taken his cue from that.

It was only right that she had as clear a second choice about him as possible. On the other hand, if a vow and a wedding ring and great sex weren't enough to feel obligated to, then tossing in a few love words wouldn't be enough either.

For a man who'd run a couple of small empires profitably and made far more right decisions than wrong ones, McClain knew he hadn't exactly covered himself with glory where his wife and this marriage was concerned.

But his part was done. He'd taken enough risks and made all the mistakes he was going to. It was up to his wife to decide what happened next.

New York was big and loud and crowded. The size didn't bother Stacey, but the noise and crush of people seemed to stand out after weeks in rural Texas. The hassle of dealing with cabs made her impatient. At the ranch, she'd simply picked a vehicle and driven wherever she wanted, parked on the street—never underground or in a parking ramp—and dealt with almost nonexistent traffic.

In New York there were bars over windows, elaborate security systems, car alarms, steel doors and multiple locks. Never had she known a single door in McClain's house to be locked, and the keys to every vehicle he owned were left hanging in the ignition.

McClain ranch was a sparsely populated ocean of safety and chivalry, where cowboys touched their hat brims respectfully, addressed her as Miss McClain or Ma'am, and everyone was straightforward and friendly.

New York wasn't a place for unlocked doors, or the unwary or for people who were too open. And most people here were too rushed and pressured by the pace and the crush, too on guard, to observe the laid-back niceties common to rural and small-town Texas.

Stacey couldn't recall ever feeling this level of unease and impatience with the street-level din of traffic and noise. She'd loved the energy and vitality of the big city before, and everything had seemed so alive and interesting.

It shocked her to realize how off-putting it all was now, how overwhelming the towering buildings were. The sun didn't shine as brightly here, and it wasn't only because the mammoth buildings blocked a lot of it.

Smog and exhaust fumes were much more noticeable to her, but perhaps they only seemed more exaggerated because she'd adapted so quickly to the clear though sometimes dusty air of rural Texas. Even the pungent smell of horse and cattle manure counted for very little, since it was noticeable only in limited areas.

All in all, everything familiar and beloved to her before now seemed alien, and compared unfavorably on nearly every score with her life on McClain Ranch.

Stacey hadn't been much more comfortable with her friends. She felt as if she'd crossed over into some alternative universe. The same things weren't as interesting to her anymore. She didn't care about this art exhibit or that designer's latest collection, or about seeing the new hit show on Broadway. She was more interested in horses, cattle markets, and rain, which was an almost appalling surprise.

And she'd started thinking about babies. If there'd been a baby or a toddler anywhere, her gaze had automatically zeroed in, and she'd thought about having a child of her own...and McClain's.

The sweet mental picture of a black-haired baby boy or girl floated through her thoughts more than once, and the notion of family stirred forcefully. Consequently, the longer she was in New York, the more she realized she didn't want to raise a child in the city, not when she could raise him or her on McClain Ranch. And her child would never be sent off to boarding school as she'd been.

When Stacey realized how far her mental plans

had gone, she was a little shocked. Particularly since she'd been in New York for five days and McClain had yet to put in an appearance. His claim of not being able to get away had seemed more flimsy every time she thought about it.

At first, she'd felt a little hurt, but then it had dawned on her what might be going on, and her upset calmed. She hadn't talked to Oren since yesterday afternoon, and she wouldn't now until she could do it face-to-face.

It was her deep, deep need to be with him again and to straighten out a few last things between them, that drove her now. That and the idea of babies.

She'd dealt with all the things in New York that needed to be dealt with at this point. The moment she was free, she caught a taxi, picked up her luggage from her hotel, then settled back to endure the aggravation of traffic delays.

Oren had had a hell of a day with the gelding. He'd come to the house and showered, eaten another solitary supper, then gone off to a cattleman's meeting. His problems with the horse were his fault. He was too distracted to work with such a volatile animal, so he'd eventually stopped before he managed to undo the tiny bit of progress he'd made.

He'd tried to reach Stacey all day, but he'd finally been told that she'd checked out of her hotel that morning. It was possible she'd decided to stay with friends. He'd tried a number of times before and after that to get her on her cell phone, but his calls went right into voice mail each time, so she must not have had it turned on.

Maybe he ought to get used to the idea that he couldn't have access to her anytime he liked. He hadn't been able to tell much about how things had gone with her friends, because she'd seemed evasive whenever he'd asked.

She'd seemed more interested in reporting on her business. Of course, part of that might have been because he'd been just as evasive with her about what he was doing with his time once the sale was over and he'd got home from the board meeting. He hadn't exactly lied about not being able to get to New York yesterday, but using the cattleman's meeting tonight had been a pretty thin excuse.

They were both doing a little dancing, and that seemed significant to him. It wasn't a good sign. He'd almost called the airlines to see if she'd booked a flight back to Texas, but he'd decided that was going too far. He wasn't going to check up on her or track her behind her back. She'd either chose to keep him informed, or she wouldn't.

Just as she could stay with him forever if she wanted. Or not.

It was after nine by the time he got back from the cattleman's meeting and let himself into the silent house. When he stepped into the foyer, he caught sight of a paper scrap on the edge of the foyer table and another one on the floor by the table leg. Curious, he walked over to set his dress Stetson on the table, but when he started to pick up the paper scraps, he saw that there was a single red rose petal beside each bit of paper.

The note beside the petal on the table read *He loves me.*

The spark of excitement he felt made him smile. The tension in his body relaxed into a sweet feeling of pleasure. Stacey was home. He bent to pick up the other note and rose petal.

He loves me not.

That one leveled his smile. Now he straightened and glanced down the hall. From here, he could see other paper scraps and rose petals strewn along the carpet. Intrigued, he left the first two notes and rose petals on the table to see where the others led. He paused over those first few and saw the alternating messages.

He loves me… He loves me not…

It was the old lovers game, only this time using red rose petals instead of the traditional daisy petals. A little tickled by the whimsy, but now roiling inside with the need to see her, Oren tried to resist the impulse to leave the paper-and-petal trail and go straight to their bedroom.

He knew he'd find her there, but because she'd gone to this much trouble—how long had it taken her to write out each little note?—he'd do everything the way she must have wanted. The last thing he'd do was spoil this for her. Or spoil it for *himself.*

It took more effort than he'd thought to patiently stick to the trail of paper scraps and rose petals and not take a shortcut. They wound through the house, through the living room into the hall, then along the carpet to the east wing. At every opportunity along the rose-petal-and-paper path, an extra *He loves me* had been placed on a tabletop, with yet another *He loves me not* on the floor beneath.

He'd more than gotten the message. Stacey didn't know whether he loved her or not, and the many notes and petals suggested an almost endless preoccupation with the question. He'd understood in particular the happy message of the highly placed *He loves me* notes, and the correspondingly low, *He loves me not* ones on the floor.

He loves me… He loves me not. High and happy…or… down and sad.

The rising feeling of joy was unlike anything

he'd ever felt before, but it intensified when he turned the corner into the east wing of the house and saw soft light spill out from their bedroom. At last Oren reached their room and walked in.

Stacey was lying on her stomach across their big bed, with literal handfuls of red rose petals scattered around her. She was propped on her elbows, focused on the task as she plucked petals, one by one, off a long-stemmed red rose. Though he couldn't hear her voice from where he stood, he could read her lips as she plucked one petal, then another.

"He loves me not, He loves me, He loves me not."

As Oren walked slowly closer, her blue, blue gaze lifted to meet his. Now the scent of roses was particularly strong. The satin nightie she had on was a new one, a delicate pink, and the V in the front went so deep that she was lying on the bottom of it. Not that he cared where it dipped to, because the choice cleavage it framed before it went out of sight was far more interesting to him.

Stacey pushed herself up and sat back on her heels in the center of the bed to give him a gentle smile. "Did you get my message?"

McClain walked close and braced a knee on the mattress to lean down and stretch out on his side across the bottom of the bed. The rose petals he'd crushed into the bedspread thickened the air even more with the rich scent. He propped his lean jaw on a fist to look at her.

''I got every one of 'em, darlin','' he drawled, and Stacey couldn't miss the smoldering heat in his gaze. ''But I've lost track of where you are with those rose petals,'' he said as he nodded toward her denuded flower stem.

Stacey struggled to keep from throwing herself into his arms. She'd missed him unbearably, but hadn't allowed herself to realize just how much until this second. If she had, she'd have booked herself on a return flight the moment her plane from Texas had landed in New York.

Every moment and every day away from McClain had been a test of her ability to resist the urge to come back early. She'd had business to take care of, and one of the things she'd vowed to do was follow through on things, whatever the cost.

It took even more self-control now to take this romantic little game all the way to the goal. She'd waited long enough to settle this, and she wasn't going to let either of them off the hook until they'd done it.

Particularly since this marriage was no longer even remotely about money, however it had begun. She'd decided it might be just as well that neither of them had ever said the words—particularly her—because when she declared herself now, McClain would be sure that she had no other motive for saying it but love.

She knew by now that for McClain, everything he'd done from the beginning had only been about love, though he'd never said the words. Would he say them now?

The wild, wild craving to be held by him prompted her to start them toward the prize.

"I'm not sure it matters if we lost track of whether this petal is a 'loves me' or a 'loves me not,' one," she said quietly.

"Sure it does," he said, then reached for the untouched long-stemmed rose beside her. He raised up a little on his elbow to angle the stem for a quick whiff of more fragrance before he held it away to study it. He rolled the stem between a finger and a thumb, then stopped to select a petal and tenderly pull it free.

His dark eyes shifted meaningfully to meet hers. "She loves me." He dropped that petal on the space between them, then plucked the next petal. "She loves me not."

That one he tossed carelessly off the edge of the bed as if dismissing it, and Stacey couldn't help her giggle. He smoothly worked his way around and around the blossom, repeating the saying with each one. Every "She loves me not," got tossed to the floor until only a single petal remained.

"I reckon this one is supposed to somehow predict and ensure that you'll tell me you love me. Just like that last one of yours predicts and ensures that I'll tell you I love you," he said, then grinned. "I already know the one you're holding is the 'loves me' petal, so you ended up with the right one."

Stacey felt a fresh burst of excitement. She'd already known her last one was the "He loves me" petal, and what Oren had just said was a confirmation that the silly game had indeed brought out an...*almost* confession.

But the disappointing thing was she also knew that Oren's last rose petal was not a "She loves me," but a "She loves me not." Stacey tried not to let it dim the fun between them.

As if he'd guessed what she was thinking, Oren chuckled. "I'll bet you've been keeping track of my rose. And from where you're sitting, it looks like this last petal is the "She loves me not" one. I reckon you're bound to be disappointed. Unless it's true that you don't love me."

"Oh, Oren, this was just a silly thing to do, just a foolish way to start something. It doesn't matter that you ended up with the 'loves me not' one for my feelings, because I *do* love you. And I've been waiting so long to tell you.''

She set aside her rose stem to move close to him, but he held up a hand to stop her.

''Look here, baby,'' he said as he playfully held up the stem with the single petal, turning it a little so she could see it better.

What she saw was that the last petal wasn't really the last one, because there were two. They overlapped each other so closely that they'd only looked like a single petal. McClain had been teasing her.

''She loves me not,'' he recited as he pulled it off and dropped it over the edge of the bed.

''She loves me.'' He plucked that last petal, but tucked it in his shirt pocket before he flipped the empty stem over his shoulder to the carpet.

''Now take that 'He loves me' petal off yours and put it in my pocket with mine.''

Stacey took her last petal, paused to toss her empty stem behind McClain, and hoped it went all the way past the foot of the bed to the floor with the one he'd tossed there. But when she moved close to him to put her last petal with his, he waited until her fingers were in his pocket before he pressed his hand over hers to gently trap it against his chest.

''I'm in love with you, darlin', and I have been

since the first time I saw you,'' he began. ''I walked into that swanky New York party and someone introduced me to a beautiful little blonde. She looked up into my eyes, put out her cool little hand and let me take it, then she smiled and said 'Welcome to New York, Mr. McClain.' I fell flat in love.''

Now he lifted her fingers to his mouth and tenderly kissed them, never looking away from her eyes. ''And I'm still in love with you, darlin'. I reckon I always will be.''

Stacey's eyes actually began to sting, and it was all she could do to keep back happy tears.

''Oh, Oren, I love you. I was so...thrilled that night. I'd never met anyone like you. I think now that I did fall in love with you then, but I didn't believe in love at first sight and I was terrified and overwhelmed by what I did feel.''

She couldn't help the emotions that were swelling so high, emotions that were a combination of love and joy with a touch of regret as she remembered how foolishly she'd turned down his first marriage proposal.

''I felt bad for turning you down that first time, and then you came back in my life when I needed someone and I knew I didn't deserve a second chance. I knew I was fond of you, but I couldn't let myself believe what I really felt. I couldn't get over how much you overwhelmed me, and yet I still made the selfish, cold-blooded decision to let you rescue me.''

She felt her eyes fill with happy tears. ''Maybe it was the pressure of what I felt for you that truly overwhelmed me, because the more I let myself realize I was in love with you, the less overwhelmed I felt.''

Stacey managed a trembling smile. ''I love you so much, Oren, so much. But…'' she let the silence stretch for a handful of quick moments before she added, ''I'm beginning to wonder if we're *ever* going to stop talking and if you're *ever* going to kiss me. It feels like ages since I've been in your arms.''

McClain's smile abruptly fell away and his rugged face took on a sudden seriousness. ''I thought you'd never get to that part, Mrs. McClain.''

They were suddenly in each other's arms, rolling in rose petals, devouring each other with kisses until Oren suddenly flinched, tore his mouth from her to hiss out a minor swear word, then lay very still. Sometime between the time they'd started and this moment, he'd lost most of his clothes. Stacey had only the short satin nightie to lose and it had probably slithered off the edge of the mattress in the first moments.

Now Oren slid his arm from around her to reach

behind his back—or rather, his backside. A moment later, he lifted the rose stem Stacey thought she'd tossed off the foot of the bed.

McClain gave her a narrow look that was filled with mock reproof before he pitched the stem away.

"Remind me to check the carpet before we go waltzing in to the shower in a little while."

And then he was kissing her again, and it turned out to be a long, very long, time before either of them were ready to think about anything but pleasuring each other.

There'd be at least fifty or sixty years of nights like this one, but it would only be another month before the morning sickness began. Once they realized what might be going on, they'd count the days and they'd realize that tonight had been the start of at least one more wonderful thing between them than they'd known about.

Their happiness together might have been complete when that first baby boy arrived, but those next years taught them that the boundaries of happiness in the McClain household were destined to expand regularly every two years or so, until three little black-haired baby boys had come into their lives.

Then there was the surprise baby sister who came along about the time the youngest of the rowdy McClain boys had started kindergarten. And that clever little dark-haired baby girl figured out the moment the nurse placed her in her daddy's arms that she was the apple of her daddy's eye.

Harlequin Romance®

A wedding dilemma:

What should a sexy, successful bachelor do if he's too busy making millions to find a wife? Or if he finds the perfect woman, and just has to strike a bridal bargain...

The perfect proposal:

The solution? For better, for worse, these grooms in a hurry have decided to sign, seal and deliver the ultimate marriage contract...to buy a bride!

Will these paper marriages blossom into wedded bliss?

Look out for our next Contract Brides story in Harlequin Romance®:

Bride of Convenience by Susan Fox—#3788

On sale March 2004

Available wherever Harlequin books are sold.

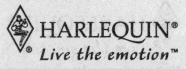

HARLEQUIN®
Live the emotion™

Visit us at www.eHarlequin.com

HRBOCSF

The world's bestselling romance series.

HARLEQUIN®
Presents

Seduction and Passion Guaranteed!

GREEK TYCOONS

**They're the men who have
everything—except a bride...**

Wealth, power, charm—what else could
a heart-stoppingly handsome tycoon need?
In the GREEK TYCOONS miniseries you have
already been introduced to some gorgeous
Greek multimillionaires who are in need of wives.

THE GREEK TYCOON'S SECRET CHILD
by Cathy Williams
on sale now, #2376

THE GREEK'S VIRGIN BRIDE
by Julia James
on sale March, #2383

THE MISTRESS PURCHASE
by Penny Jordan
on sale April, #2386

Pick up a Harlequin Presents® novel and you will
enter a world of spine-tingling passion and
provocative, tantalizing romance!

Available wherever Harlequin books are sold.

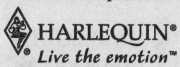

HARLEQUIN®
Live the emotion™

Visit us at www.eHarlequin.com

HPGT2004

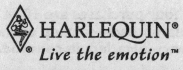

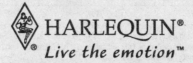

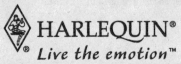

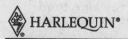

Coming Next Month

#3791 THE DUKE'S PROPOSAL Sophie Weston
Supermodel Jemima Dare needs to get away from it all.
Traveling incognito, she flees to a Caribbean paradise in
search of peace. But there's no peace to be found with
Niall Blackthorne around! He's aristocratic, irresistible—
and a danger to Jemima's heart!

#3792 MISSION: MARRIAGE Hannah Bernard
Lea is turning thirty and the alarm on her biological
clock is ringing. But how does a woman with just one
ex-boyfriend learn to find Mr. Right? Tom is a serial
dater, with no interest in settling down—but he's
perfect as a dating consultant! Except their "practice
date" leads to more than one "practice kiss."

#3793 THE MAN FROM MADRID Anne Weale
Cally hoped for peace and quiet when she escaped to Valdecarras-
ca in beautiful rural Spain—but the arrival of mysterious millionaire Nicolás Llorca changed all that!
Nicolás has made it clear he's not looking for long-term commitment…but he's made an offer Cally can't resist!

#3794 A WEDDING AT WINDEROO Barbara Hannay
Piper O'Malley has always come to Gabe for advice.
So, after she discovers she's going to lose her home
unless she gets married, who better to teach her the
art of flirtation? Gabe agrees to give her some tips on
how to attract men, but the unexpected chemistry
between them takes them both by surprise!

HRCNM0304